The Ghost of Dibble Hollow

By MAY NICKERSON WALLACE

Illustrated by ORIN KINCADE

Cover by DOM LUPO

SCHOLASTIC BO

NEW YORK • LONDON • RICHMOND HILL, ONTARIO

Mona Rummel

To MURIEL FULLER

2nd printing .... May 1965

Printed in the U.S.A.

Contents

CHAPTER 1

Dibble Hollow

"I'M GOING OVER to look at those old guns," Pug Allen told his sister Helen. He pointed to the war memorial on Smithville's village green, where a boy about his own age — thirteen — was sitting astride one of the cannons.

"You'd better stay here by the car, Pug," Helen said. "Mom and Dad won't be more than a few minutes getting the key for Dibble Hollow and we want to go the minute they get back."

"They said we could stretch our legs," Pug reminded her. "It's been a long ride from Fairtown. Besides, I have to walk Ricky."

"Walk Ricky! Look!" Helen cried. "He's already out there — chasing chickens!"

Pug saw with horror that his sister was right. His half-grown beagle was barking and snapping at the tail feathers of several brown hens fanning out across the park-like green. A young girl was desperately trying to round up the hens and catch them. Ricky pretended not to hear as Pug raced toward him calling a sharp command. The dog continued to struggle even when Pug caught him at last and shut him up in the Allen's station wagon.

Hurrying back to the chicken roundup, Pug found that Helen and the other girl, with the help of bystanders, had caught all but one of the big Rhode Island Red hens. Pug threw himself on the last runaway, and put her, still squawking, with the other hens in the coop that stood on the back of an old platform truck.

Breathless, Pug came back into the circle of interested spectators. A tall elderly man, waving his cane, finally made himself heard above the hubbub of the roundup.

"Priscilla Smith!" he boomed. "What in time happened here? Who let those hens out?" He flourished his cane at Pug. "That was your dog chasing them, I'll warrant!"

Before Pug could reply, Helen said with spirit, "We certainly didn't let them out."

But the old man looked as if he were about to explode. "That ornery dog of yours —"

"Now, Grandpa," Priscilla interrupted. "I saw Joey Pratt open the coop. Ernie Pratt was sitting on the cannon and I was carrying the groceries — and we couldn't get here soon enough to stop him."

Pug admired the way the girl stood up to her glowering grandfather. She was smaller than Helen, but seemed about the same age as his eleven-year-old sister.

"I saw that dog chase my chickens!" her grandfather replied angrily. "And nobody would let a dog run hens that way but summer people — or Dibbles!"

"Well, we *are* summer people and we *are* Dibbles," Pug declared stiffly. "My name is Elisha Nathanael Dibble Allen, and this is my sister Helen. My mother owns Dibble Hollow now and we're going to stay there all summer."

A murmur ran through the crowd that had gathered.

"Dibble Hollow!" Pug heard the name echoed several times.

"I wouldn't live there for love or money," one man said to his neighbor.

"Dibble Hollow! That's the spooky place!" said another.

Most of all Pug was amazed at the effect of his words on the old man.

His lined face grew very pale. He put his hand to his forehead and for a moment closed his eyes.

"I knew it," the old man said. His voice trembled. "I knew it. You're the spit 'n' image of Nathanael Dibble." Suddenly he turned on the crowd and brandished his cane. "All right. Move along. Come, Priscilla, get into that truck. We have hens to deliver."

"Thank you for helping me," Priscilla said softly to Pug and Helen. "We'll be neighbors — I live at Twin Maples down the road a piece from Dibble Hollow. Please don't think too bad of Grandpa." She seemed to be pleading. "He's a little upset — seeing you kind of sudden and hearing that you're Dibble."

"A *little* upset," Pug muttered to Helen as they walked back to the car. "Why is it so upsetting to see a Dibble?"

Helen looked woebegone. "Whatever it is we didn't make it any better, thanks to Ricky!" she exclaimed. "Wait till Mom and Dad hear about it!"

Mr. and Mrs. Allen heard the story gravely.

"It's unfortunate to start out like that with neighbors," Mrs. Allen said regretfully. "We'll just have to show Mr. Smith there's no ill will on our part, whatever his grudge may be against the Dibble family."

Pug thought his mother and father, and even Helen, seemed to forget the incident rather quickly. As they drove the last five miles through beautiful hill country, they exclaimed over every fresh view. But Pug was quiet. He wondered about that boy on the cannon. Ernie Pratt — wasn't that his name? What had the man in the crowd meant when he said he wouldn't live at Dibble Hollow for love or money? And what was that spooky talk?

"There it is!" Helen yelled suddenly. "That *must* be Dibble Hollow!"

The overloaded station wagon braked to a stop and they all looked out eagerly at the old white house. It looked small in the shade of the tall oaks and elms. But it looked so sturdy that Pug liked it immediately.

Before he could unwedge himself from the luggage piled around him, Helen had deposited her boxes on Pug's lap and climbed nimbly from the car. She was at the gate of the picket fence ten steps ahead of him.

"Your inheritance, Mother!" she cried dramatically. "Look! It says on the door 'Built in 1730.' O-o-oh, it does look kind of spooky!"

"Fooey," said Pug for what he called her dramatics, but he too stared curiously at the old house his mother had recently inherited from her great uncle.

"Say, maybe it's haunted or something," he said cheerfully. That might explain why a person wouldn't want to live there, he thought.

"Nonsense," Mrs. Allen said brightly. "Any house that hasn't been lived in for a time looks a little lonely. But we'll soon change that, won't we, dear?" She appealed to her husband.

Mr. Allen agreed. Then he looked around at the high weeds and the sprawling yellow bushes in the corners of the yard. "It certainly has been neglected," he observed. "You may wish you were back mowing nice short city grass for the neighbors, Pug."

"Not me," Pug said stoutly. "This suits me fine — and Ricky too." The beagle had already explored the lilacs at each side of the door, and had chased a squirrel up the large cherry tree that leaned against a corner of the house. Now the dog sniffed his way along the flowering borders back to his master.

"Yes, sir, this suits me fine," Pug repeated. "It's kind of a funny feeling to know that Dibbles have always lived here. It's almost like being away for a visit and then coming home. Come on, Mom, who has the key?"

Mr. Allen took the key from his pocket as they went up the flagstone walk.

"Look, Helen, there's even a barn behind the house!" Pug gloated. Then he stopped, puzzled. That's funny, he thought. The weathervane on the barn was whirling merrily. Yet there was not a breath of air stirring the leaves of the trees. Pug looked around quickly. His parents hadn't noticed it. But trust Helen not to miss a thing.

"Look at that!" she cried.

By the time Mr. Allen looked up, the weathervane was still.

"It was whirling," Helen insisted.

"Nothing strange if it was," said her father. "There could have been a gentle current of air at that height." He unlocked the door and threw it open. "Welcome to Dibble Hollow."

At that moment there was a loud bang upstairs, and the sound of something falling. Everyone jumped. Mr. Allen shook his head. "These country houses! There's always a loose shutter somewhere."

But Pug wondered. It would take an awfully loose shutter in a high wind to make that noise.

At first the Allens stayed together, exploring the downstairs, and opening windows in the big square living room to rid the house of the musty, unlived-in smell.

Finally, Mr. Allen dropped into a rocker and rested his head against its high back. "Praise Allah for good chairs!" he said gratefully.

"The dining room is nice too," Mrs. Allen said from the next doorway. A moment later she called back, "The kitchen is certainly old-fashioned. But I daresay this hand pump and wood drainboard and sink were pure luxury to my great-grandmother. I wonder if there's a bathroom."

Pug and Helen had already started upstairs, with Ricky at Pug's heels.

Pug knew the bedroom he wanted. He had seen the cherry tree close by the corner window.

"I want that bedroom where the cherry tree hits the house!" Pug said, two steps ahead of Helen on the stairs.

"Oh, sure, go ahead. Be a pig," she panted.

But she saw that the cherry-tree room was small and dark, and she said, "Ugh, you can have it." Looking over his shoulder she gave a little shiver. "It's — kind of eerie in here."

She ran into the other bedroom, and Pug heard her cry of delight.

The dark little bedroom just suited Pug. He liked the two single beds with the low nightstand between them. There was a high pine chest in one corner under the eaves, and a rocker in the other corner. A faded rag rug covered the wide boards between the beds, and on the beds were old-fashioned crazy quilts of many colors. An oval-framed portrait of a boy hung over one bed.

Only one thing about the room bothered Pug. Ricky would not enter it. Pug patted one of the beds invitingly. But Ricky just stood in the doorway with his ruff up, and whined. Finally Pug lost patience.

"Okay," he said. "Go ahead and sleep on the mat outside for all I care. I'm sleeping in here. This is the room I want."

Helen was thrilled with her room, and Mr. and Mrs. Allen seemed quite content with theirs.

"There *is* a bathroom," Mrs. Allen said with a sigh of relief. "I couldn't remember; I was so little when I was here last."

"I bet we won't have to take more than one bath a week here in the country," Pug said hopefully.

"Well, we all need baths today," said his father firmly. "Just as soon as we get the station wagon unloaded, in you go."

The unloading was hard work. As they took out the bicycles, Mr. Allen grunted, "Pug, if you hadn't wanted to bring these bikes there would have been more room for my books and photographic equipment."

"It was your suggestion that this should be an out-of-doors summer, Jim," Mrs. Allen reminded him.

"The bicycles were a nuisance on the trip, but I'm sure they'll be invaluable now that we're here."

"Maybe so. Come along, Pug. I'm ready for a bath right now."

By now even Pug was ready to wash. But when his turn came there was only a thin trickle of water, followed by dry coughing from the pump.

"Maybe the pump needs priming," his mother suggested.

"What do you mean?"

"I mean water poured into the mouth of the pump to bring water up. You'll have to go to the brook, Pug."

Pug went whistling to the brook to carry back a pail of water for the pump-priming job. He poured the water into the pump and tried it. It did no good. Then Mr. Allen tried the pump, but he had no success either.

"That's a fine how-do-you-do," he said in exasperation. "You don't suppose we're out of water the first day, do you?"

"Surely not." Mrs. Allen looked at him anxiously. "Maybe you'd better hunt up a plumber before noon. They may know of one at the village store."

Pug could not tell when his father returned from this errand whether he was more irritated or amused.

"Of all the stuff and nonsense," he said as he came in. "The only plumber in town is a man named Potter. If he can finish his other calls *before dark*, he'll come today — otherwise not till Monday. He says he positively won't set foot at Dibble Hollow after dark. It looks to me as if someone has given this place a pretty bad name."

"I bet it's that old Mr. Smith," Pug declared. "From the way he acted this morning when Helen and I were trying to help catch his old chickens, I wouldn't put it past him. You should have seen him waving his cane at me when he found out that I was Nathanael Dibble Allen."

"Pug," said his mother, "don't speak so rudely of Mr. Smith. He is going to be our neighbor and you could be as wrong about him as he is about you and Helen."

"But you should have heard—"

His mother cut short his criticism. "If Mr. Potter gets here today we can manage until he comes," she said. "I did draw quite a bit of water for cooking and drinking before we started on baths."

Mr. Allen looked dubious. "A few hours may be all right. But I don't see spending the summer in a house with a short water supply."

They were all glad when Mr. Potter arrived early that afternoon. He puttered around the kitchen and the cellar for an hour. Then he shook his head. "It looks as if you folks are out of water, sure enough," he said gloomily.

The Allens stared at one another in dismay.

"You mean you can't do *anything*?"

The plumber shook his head. "It looks as if the well is plumb dry," he said. "Nothing I can do. Either a well has water or it hasn't. It just goes to show you never can tell the depth of the well by the length of the handle on the pump. I'm sorry," he added. "You seem like nice folks. Too bad this place has such a jinx on it."

He was gone before anyone could ask what he meant.

Helen was in tears. Mrs. Allen looked as if she were close to crying herself. Mr. Allen jingled the coins in his pocket as he always did when he was troubled.

Pug felt as if the world had come to an end. Leave? Now? He had dreamed of living here ever since the day it became his mother's house. They couldn't give up yet.

"Why did he say there's a jinx on this place?" Pug wanted to know.

His father snorted. "Poppycock! No wonder they haven't been able to keep this place rented. There's no water!"

"Did the Dibbles have trouble with the well back in your grandfather's time?" Pug asked his mother.

"I don't think so," she answered slowly. "But I was only five, you know, when I came here that year before Grandpa Nathanael died. I can't understand it. There seemed to be more than enough water then. But I suppose wells do run dry sometimes."

"We can't go. We mustn't!" cried Helen. "Isn't there something we can do? I heard at Sunday school about a missionary who had to bring in all the water his family needed. He had to carry it in buckets from a waterhole. And then they boiled every drop they used. Couldn't we do that?"

"I'm willing to carry water from the brook if we can stay," Pug said quickly.

"I'd be glad to boil it if you and your father could haul enough for everything that has to be done," his mother replied. "But it would mean being careful of every single drop."

They all waited anxiously as Mr. Allen walked over to the window. "I don't know," he said as he looked across the green fields toward the brook. "It's a long haul from that brook. Well, we can try it the rest of the day. That'll give us an idea of what we would be up against. Personally, I don't think Pug and I would last through Sunday."

By bedtime, even Pug was not sure. He had had no idea of how hard it was to carry water nor of the amount of water a family used.

He had tried to think of himself as rescuing people in a stockade, slipping out at night to get them drinking water in spite of Indians. He had imagined he was running through crossfire in Korea, bringing water to dying comrades. But on the last trip of the evening he was just a tired American boy with dead weights at the ends of his aching arms.

"If only it were anything but a lack of water," Mrs. Allen said unhappily, "I think we could weather it. But no water! I'm very much afraid we'll have to give up."

Pug and Helen were still protesting as they went to bed.

Helen walked into Pug's room before going on to her own. "I can't bear it," she said tearfully.

Pug had thrown himself on his bed with his back against the wall, and only grunted in reply. He was in no mood to talk. Suddenly Helen said, "You know, Pug, lying there right under the picture of that boy, you look enough like him to be his brother. In fact you could almost be *him,* except for the funny clothes he's wearing."

Pug grunted again, and finally, with a sniffle, Helen left.

Ricky crept up to the door and lay with his nose on his paws, whining softly. Pug tried again to coax him inside. But Ricky would not enter the room. At last Pug patted him on the head and shut his door.

Pug had pretended no interest in Helen's remarks about him and the boy in the portrait. But now he walked over to the picture and looked at it long and closely. Golly, she could be right! There was the Dibble mouth — "cut for pie," his mother always said. And that straight straw-colored hair and pointed chin belonged to the Dibbles too. This boy must have been an ancestor of his, and this had probably been his room.

I wonder what his name was, Pug thought. Funny, there was a painting of only one boy, but there were two beds. Which had the boy slept in? Sometimes a fellow carved his initials on something of his own, way out of sight.

On an impulse. Pug lifted the pillow from the bed under the window, and pulled back the mattress. Lucky shot in the dark, he thought excitedly. Low on the headboard were gouged crooked letters spelling out the name "Miles Dibble." Quickly Pug investigated the other bed, and found in even cruder letters "Nathanael." So! There had been two boys.

Very pleased with his discovery, Pug crawled into Miles' bed. Long after the lights were out in the rest of the house and everything had quieted down he lay staring into the darkness. If only he could figure out some way to get water from the brook, they might be able to stay.

The moon had risen. It shone through the gable window, lighting the portrait. But what was happening to the quilt on the other bed? Why was it shimmering? Suddenly Pug realized that he was seeing the quilt through a strange mist. And it wasn't moonlight! Little by little as he stared the mist grew denser. It thickened and wavered. And then before his unbelieving eyes it assumed the shape of a boy sitting cross-legged on the bed.

CHAPTER 2

The Ghost of Dibble Hollow

Pug CLOSED HIS EYES — tightly — and opened them again. The boy was still there. Slowly Pug's eyes traveled upward from the high-top button boots, to the striped stockings which disappeared under straight pant legs that came to just below the knees. The pants he wore were fastened at the waist with two buttons on each side. That is, one side had buttons and the other side was held together with a piece of string. The boy had on a white shirt and a bow tie, and there was no doubt about it — the mischievous face was the same as that in the painting.

"I would be obliged to you," the boy said, "if you would sleep in this bed hereafter."

It could not be just his imagination, Pug told himself. Not if this ghostly figure spoke. He decided to say something too.

"H-Hello," he said. "Why should I sleep over there?"

"Because you are in *my* bed now, as I should think you could have seen for yourself when you pulled back the tick and saw the headboard where I carved my name when I was ten. I am Miles Dibble."

"Miles Dibble!" said Pug. "Yes, I found the name all right, but I didn't know whether the painting over there was of Miles or Nathanael. I knew it looked something like me so I figured it must be a Dibble."

"I know," said Miles. "A Dibble is a Dibble and there's no getting away from it."

"I don't mind," Pug replied. "I'm kind of proud of it." He paused. "But that outfit you're wearing is a riot."

"What do you mean 'a riot'?"

"I mean — well, funny."

Miles' eyes turned suddenly angry.

Pug was surprised. "For Pete's sake, I didn't mean anything," he said quickly. "I guess that's what boys wore in your day. But I wouldn't want to be caught dead in those clothes myself."

"You could scarcely help it if that is what you happened to be wearing when you died," Miles retorted. "Okay, let it pass. I accept your apology."

Pug was glad to let the matter drop right there, but Miles suddenly went on with it. "Maybe I do look a little fancy in that picture," he admitted. "Aunt Maria painted it after I was gone. She sent it clear over to Milltown to have it framed in a real store-bought frame," he added proudly. "She never thought of me as too good to live while I was alive, I can tell you. She taught at old Number Four School, and she gave me more than one swat on the seat of my britches when I played hooky to go fishing with Eb Smith." He laughed silently. "She told Ma we were imps of Satan and would come to no good end. Then after I was gone, she painted me in my best bib and tucker, looking like a plaster saint. A good likeness if I do say so myself." He laughed again. "But she was nearer the bull's-eye when she said I would come to no good end."

"You're really Miles' ghost!"

"Naturally — or I should say supernaturally." Miles seemed pleased with his joke. "What else would I be when I am dead? Criminentlies!"

"Criminentlies?"

"Well, we were not allowed to swear when Ma was around," Miles explained. "But a fellow has to have something he can say to let off steam."

"Miles," Pug asked suddenly. "Have you been scaring people away from Dibble Hollow?"

"I may truthfully say I am largely responsible," Miles acknowledged modestly. "But of course you can make nearly anyone turn tail and run if he sees something he does not understand."

"Like what?"

"Like spinning weathercocks and banging blinds." Miles winked.

"I knew there was something funny about that. What else can you do?"

"Oh, I can make chairs rock." Miles snapped his fingers and the low rocker began to creak back and forth.

Pug gulped. "What else?"

"I can make your hair stand on end."

"You're fooling."

"Am I?" Miles cocked his thumb in Pug's direction. Pug felt a slight shock and with the crackle of static electricity, every hair on his head stood straight out as stiff as so many straws. Miles jerked back his hand and Pug's hair flipped down to his scalp again.

"Wow, that's a neat trick," Pug said admiringly. "Can you grant wishes?"

"I am a ghost — not a genie out of a bottle," Miles reminded him with dignity. "But I can play the mouth organ." He whipped out an old harmonica which he wiped on his britches. He paused with the instrument raised to his mouth. "Eb Smith said I could never carry a tune in a basket. But listen."

Pug winced. He clapped his hands over his ears as Miles played. "Is Eb Smith that old Grandpa Smith at Twin Maples?" he asked.

Miles nodded. "He always said I had a tin ear."

"He sure is right on *that*," Pug said. "Hey — don't make so much noise," he warned as Miles raised the

mouth organ to his lips again. "Mom and Dad will hear you."

"They cannot hear me."

"You mean that? They're lucky! But why not?" Pug asked curiously.

"No one can hear me or see me except a Dibble boy like me — under fifteen, that is — and one other person, who is very special to me."

The two studied each other. Pug was so full of questions he did not know where to start.

"Was Nathanael — the one in that bed over there — my grandfather?"

"Yes, he was my little brother. You look just like him."

"I was named for him."

"I am aware of it, though I heard your mother call you Pug. Very repugnant!" He held his nose between his thumb and first finger, but he grinned and Pug laughed with him.

"Miles," Pug said soberly. "I love it here, but we'll probably have to move out like the others before us. We're in a jam!"

"That is why I appeared tonight instead of waiting to know you better," Miles told him. Reluctantly he put away his mouth organ. "I was afraid the apparent lack of water would drive you away. I could not let a Dibble family go when I have been waiting so many years for the right Dibble to come."

"Why did you try to stop us then with that goofy weathervane trick and the banging shutter?"

"I did not know who you were at first. As soon as you came in I saw you were the spit 'n' image of Nathanael. I could not let you go then."

He held up his hand as Pug started to ask a question. "I will tell you *why* later. The important thing now is that you are here. I do not want you to leave."

"You said apparent lack of water," Pug got back to their problem. "You mean there *is* water?"

"Your ancestors were not idiots," Miles said with dignity. "They had to have water too, you know. If one well was too shallow, they dug another."

"But where? There's only one pump."

"If piping were scarce as hen's teeth and cost a lot, where would you put a second well?"

Pug thought. "Where it could be connected to the first one?" he ventured.

"Right." Miles leaned forward. "Listen. Tomorrow go down cellar to the wall under the piping in the kitchen. Pace toward the brook and dig in the cellar floor about a foot to the right —" He paused and looked at his hands with a frown. "Well just to be safe, dig about a foot to the right *and* to the left of the pipe going up to the sink pump. I do not just remember whether it is right or left, but you will unearth a big horizontal pipe and a wheel. I fancy you will not be able to turn it even with a wrench, but maybe your father can. It will open the valve and let in water from the reserve well. And that well will not run dry."

"Why was the connection turned off?"

"After my father and your grandfather died, my

oldest brother Ezra did not want company. He buried the connecting pipe and gave out the story that the homestead was water-shy. His grandson, the one who left the place to your mother, never did know there was an extra well."

"Jeepers, Miles. If I can find that wheel, we'll get to stay the rest of the summer the way we planned! Wait till I tell the family about you. They'll —"

"That you must never do! If you say one word about me you can be sure you will never see me again."

"Don't go," Pug begged in alarm. "Okay, I won't breathe a word about you! But how will I explain how I knew that the wheel connection was buried in the cellar?"

"You'll think of something if you put your mind to it. Now, good night. You must be up with the lark."

"Hey — wait — wait —"

Pug wanted to know much more, but Miles had melted into the moonlight over the bed.

Pug rubbed his eyes. There was nothing but the stream of moonlight spilling into the room. Had he been dreaming with his eyes open? His mother sometimes accused him of that. After all it had been a long, hard day. His father would say he was wound up and imagining things because he was overtired. Or that Helen's talk about the portrait just before he went to bed had made the boy in the painting come alive in his thoughts. Maybe he had been dreaming. Dreams could be so vivid that they sometimes seemed real.

Whether Miles was ghost or dream, it could not

hurt to dig up the cellar floor under the kitchen sink.
Pug wished he could go down right that minute but,
of course, he would make too much noise. The house
already had a restless, sleepless feeling. He could hear
Helen's bed creak as she turned over. What would he
tell the family if there were nothing in the cellar? For
that matter, what would he tell them if there were?
Pug did not see how he could wait until morning.

CHAPTER 3

The Well

WHEN PUG OPENED HIS EYES, sunshine was streaming in through the cherry tree branches. It took him a moment or two to get his bearings. This strange place was Dibble Hollow. Then he remembered Miles. He shook his head. In the bright morning sunlight the recollection seemed more like a dream than ever.

Pug had intended to be up much earlier, but even now no one else in the house was stirring. He dressed very quietly and carried his shoes downstairs. Ricky was in the kitchen. The dog scratched frantically at the door when he saw his master going out. Pug decided to carry some water from the brook for breakfast use before he started to explore the cellar. Delightedly Ricky scampered beside him.

"The truth is I'm scared to look for that pipe, Rick," Pug told the dog as he filled the pails. "This morning the whole idea seems nutty. Well, come on, boy, let's get something to dig with and find out."

Pug found a spade in the barn. With his flashlight playing a feeble beam of light before him, he tiptoed down the steep open steps to the gloomy cellar. He paused at the foot of the stairway sniffing the damp, earthy smell. Something moved in the preserve cupboard across the basement. Ricky whined.

Pug laughed shakily. "You little fake," he half whispered. "A mouse stamps his feet at you and you run. Never mind, I almost bolted up the stairs myself."

He turned to the wall on the brook side of the house and located the pipes under the sink. So far, so good. Then he began to dig. He dug both to the right and to the left of the pipes for what seemed a very long time. It was hard work. The earth floor was solidly packed. He must be crazy to think he had seen and talked to a boy named Miles Dibble, or even dreamed of him. He leaned on the spade, flexed his tingling hands, and panted from his exertion.

"Ricky," said Pug, "do you believe in ghosts?"

He looked around. Ricky had not come down with him at all. The dog was still at the top of the steps, with his ruff raised the way it was when he met a strange dog. He wagged his tail when Pug spoke, but he stayed where he was.

Pug laughed. "Boy, you *are* a coward. Come down and help. We'll give it one more try."

He heard his mother's steps in the kitchen and started to dig again as quietly as possible. In a moment he heard the sound of metal on metal. He had struck something. His heart thumped. He went on digging quickly. And then he saw it — something that looked like a wheel for opening a valve. It was connected to a pipe.

"Criminentlies!" said a voice in his ear. "I thought you would never find it!"

Pug jumped almost a foot. There was Miles leaning over the trench with him.

Ricky began to growl and then to whine again. Mrs. Allen opened the door and called to him.

"How did you get there, Rick? I thought I put you in the kitchen last night." She started hesitantly down the step past the dog. She quickened her pace as Pug shouted, "Mom! Mom!"

Miles had disappeared, murmuring, "One-two, skidoo-oo-oo!"

"Pug, whatever are you doing down here?" his mother asked. "Are you all right?"

She saw him kneeling beside the trench and ran toward him. She looked into the trench and said, "What is it?"

It was his father who answered. "It's a connection for a valve to shut off liquid or gas."

Pug was as startled as his mother to hear Mr. Allen's voice. He had been too excited to hear his father and Helen running down the stairs.

Mr. Allen dropped to his knees to examine the piping more closely. "I'm no mechanical engineer, but it certainly looks as if you had got hold of something important, Pug," he said. He rose and brushed the damp earth from his knees. "We'd better get Mr. Potter over as soon as he can come. He'll have the proper tools to work with. We don't want to ruin anything through ignorance."

There was such a to-do about getting in touch with Mr. Potter that no one questioned Pug immediately about his discovery. Mr. Potter said he was leaving for church and would come later in the day.

It was not until they sat down to lunch that Mrs. Allen asked the question Pug had known would come sooner or later: "What in the world made you dig down there?"

Pug was glad he had thought out an explanation.

"Well, I kind of figured there must be more water somewhere if there had been plenty when you were a little girl visiting here," he answered. "And since it didn't look much different in the kitchen than you remembered, it had to be something connected with the pipes there." That was true, Pug reflected. It was exactly what Miles' questioning had led him to think.

"Of course we won't know until Mr. Potter gets here whether it means more water," Mr. Allen reminded them, accepting Pug's answer at its face value.

"H'm," was all Mr. Potter said when he first examined the connection. "H'm." Then after a moment,

"Well, now, it could be. It could very well be. Come to think of it, I never heard my grandfather tell about this place being short of water."

As he unpacked his plumber's tools, he said to Pug, "What's the matter with your dog?"

Ricky was standing at the top of the cellar stairs, whining.

"He's afraid of ghosts," Pug said, innocently.

"Pug!" Mr. Allen rebuked him. "Let's not have any nonsense."

Mr. Potter hesitated with a wrench in hand. Then he laughed a little uncertainly, said something about "kids' jokes," and turned his attention to his work.

"One of you go up and pour water into the pump to prime her," he directed when the wheel finally turned.

Pug ran to do his bidding. Pitcherful after pitcherful he poured into the thirsty pump, working the handle as he did so. At first there was only the sound of air. Then the pump handle became harder and harder to work.

"It's coming!" Pug yelled. "I can feel water coming!"

As the others clattered up the stairs, water gushed from the mouth of the pump. It was very dirty water at first, but finally it cleared.

"What do you know!" said Mr. Potter. "It looks as if you folks got yourself an extra well. Well now, I'm mighty glad. Dibble Hollow wouldn't hardly be Dibble Hollow without a Dibble, would it?" He laughed heartily at his joke as he put his tools away.

On the side porch Mr. Potter stopped and looked down the road toward the village. The Twin Maples chimney tops were just visible against the green slopes and more distant blue hills.

"I hope there won't be any trouble between you folks and Eb Smith," he said. "I heard about the ruckus on the green in Smithville yesterday morning when you first came. Eb Smith raised his cane and threatened you, eh?"

"The children told us about it," Mr. Allen said quickly. "They were trying to help Priscilla Smith catch some of Mr. Smith's chickens. They'd gotten out of a coop and were running wild — with Ricky's help, I'm sorry to say."

Mr. Potter nodded. "I heard it was one of the blasted little Pratt kids that let the chickens out before their big brother Ernie could stop them," he said. "But Eb figured it had to be a Dibble if a Dibble was in stone's throw. I hear he most had a stroke when he saw Nathanael here, the spit 'n' image of old Nathanael that was." He swallowed and went on. "Eb is old and he's mighty crochety. No use trying to gainsay that. He's been feeding this Dibble-Smith grudge so long it's got to be kind of a pet of his. You might even say he enjoys fattening it. Well, my wife would tell me I'm butting into what's none of my business, but — well —"

"There won't be any trouble with Mr. Smith as far as we're concerned," Mrs. Allen assured him. She pushed her fair hair back from her forehead and looked questioningly at Mr. Potter. "I'm afraid I don't know much about this feud or what started it in the first place."

Mr. Potter had walked down the steps. He turned at the bottom to look back at them.

"Looks as if the original trouble kind of got itself lost in the shuffle." He shook his head. "I don't suppose anybody knows exactly what happened except Eb Smith himself. Or maybe old Miss Fanny Woodman. Or Miles Dibble. And *he* can't tell anything, 'tisn't likely — being dead over fifty years." He looked around quickly.

Pug was glad everyone was watching Mr. Potter, for he could not help a little gasp at the mention of Miles.

"Miles and Eb were like brothers once," Mr. Potter went on. "There's plenty of stories, of course, about what happened. Seems as if it was something about some money the Smiths think the Dibbles did them out of when Eb was a boy."

He got as far as his car before he turned again.

"Reason I said what I did about hoping you folks wouldn't have any trouble with Eb is because he's worse'n ever about it lately. Kind of off his rocker." He hesitated. "Eb had to take out a mortgage on his farm when his daughter-in-law took sick and died leaving Prissy with him. She's the granddaughter you and Pug were trying to help," he said to Helen, who was listening open-mouthed. "For one reason or another he's never been able to get the dern thing paid off. And the money he thinks the Dibbles took would go a long ways toward covering it. So they say," he finished with an embarrassed laugh.

"I'm sure no Dibble ever took anyone's money," Mrs. Allen said. "But I'm terribly sorry about Mr. Smith's troubles." She looked genuinely distressed.

"I just thought you ought to know how things stand," Mr. Potter told her cheerfully. "Helps sometimes to figure why people do the things they do." He waved his hand and got into his car, leaning out for the last word. "This old homestead sure looks peaceful in the daytime with Dibbles in it. Makes a person wonder how it got such a reputation for being haunted, don't it? You folks seen anything funny going on around here since you come?"

Mr. Allen shook his head. Mrs. Allen and Helen laughingly shook theirs too.

"It beats the Dutch how tales do spread," Mr. Potter said and waved a final good-bye.

Pug was glad no one had noticed him. He rejoiced too soon, however, for Helen was definitely suspicious about the well. When Mr. Potter had gone and Pug was heading for his room Helen caught up with him.

"Where are you going?" she asked.

"What's it to you?"

"You know some secret about this house," she accused him. "You needn't try to act innocent with me, Pug Allen."

"Oh, go fly a kite."

"I want to know how you knew where to look for that well."

"Maybe I dreamed where it was."

"Haha. Do you know any more funny ones?"

"What's so funny about that?" He looked at her speculatively. "Okay. Maybe it wasn't all my own idea. Yeah, when you said I looked like that boy in the picture over the bed, you probably helped."

"How could that have anything to do with it?"

"I was looking at the painting just before I went to bed so I guess I dreamed about him. You wouldn't believe me if I said his ghost told me where to find water, would you?"

"Ha!"

Her scoffing tone reassured him.

"So I dreamed he told me there used to be another well. And where would it be except hitched up to the other one?"

"Oh, Pug, maybe what I said did make you dream it. Isn't it exciting?"

She started off and turned back. "You're sure you didn't find any old papers or anything?"

"When would I have had time? I've been carrying water ever since we got here."

She nodded, satisfied.

Pug went on up to his room and shut the door. Helen's harping on the theme of old papers or a diary had given him another idea. Mr. Potter had said Mr. Smith or Miles Dibble would know the cause of the

Dibble-Smith feud. He certainly was not going to find out anything from Mr. Smith — not after that run-in they had with him. But what if Miles had known? What if he had hidden what he knew right here in his room? Where else would a fellow hide something he wanted to keep to himself?

The room must have been cleaned hundreds of times since Miles had slept in it. But Pug knew there were ways of keeping things to oneself if one wanted to. This was all solid, heavy furniture; there were plenty of places to hide things.

He was looking under the mattress of Miles' bed when there was a sharp rap on the door. Helen came right in without waiting for an invitation. She carried an armful of clean shorts and T-shirts.

"What do you mean barging in here?" Pug asked, startled.

"Mother had these clothes in her suitcase and she asked me to take them to you. I had a perfect right."

"You're supposed to wait when you knock."

"What difference does it make unless you're hiding something? What did you find?" she asked eagerly.

"Nothing, snoopy. Just exactly nothing."

"Well, what were you looking for?"

"Nothing."

"Nice you found it," she said sarcastically. She came over and raised the pillow and mattress that Pug had dropped back into place. "Miles Dibble," she read the name carved low on the headboard.

"Why, Pug, he's one of the Dibbles Mr. Potter

mentioned. I know what *I'm* going to do. I'm going to find out about the trouble between the Smiths and the Dibbles because I want to get to know Priscilla. She seemed awfully nice even if we did meet under horrow- horrow —"

"Harrowing," said Pug.

"Harrowing circumstances," Helen went on. "All on account of your dog, I might add."

"So, how are you going to do this — this sleuthing?"

"First off I'm going to see what mother knows about Miles and then I'm going to see Miss Woodman."

Pug looked at her as if she had lost her mind.

"You're what? You mean go over to talk to a stranger? Are you crazy?"

"Well, we're Dibbles, aren't we? Who has a better right to know what it's all about?"

"You'd better ask Mom. It sounds awfully nosy to me."

"It's not nosy! Father always says to get to the bottom of a rumor. Track it down before you judge anyone, he says."

Helen flounced out and Pug followed her into his mother's bedroom where Mrs. Allen was making the bed.

"Mother, who was Miles Dibble?" Helen asked.

"Let me see. Grandfather Nathanael had two brothers. The one I heard most about was his older brother Ezra. Miles was probably the boy who died when he was quite young." She plumped the pillows before adding, "My father died when I was very little, the same year as Grandfather Nathanael, so I never knew much about my Dibble ancestors."

"We'd like to find out about them. Can we take our bikes and go see Miss Woodman?"

"Well, I can't see any harm in it if you're polite about it. How will you find out where she lives?"

"At the village store and post office."

"It won't be open this afternoon — not on Sunday. But you may go tomorrow, and if you get that far, please bring home two more loaves of bread. I'd forgotten that good fresh air and exercise could whip up such appetites. This summer is going to do us good, now that we've found water."

She kissed Helen's pink cheek lightly.

"Remember, if Miss Woodman is busy or doesn't want to talk, don't pester her," she cautioned them once more.

CHAPTER 4

Tiger

HELEN AND PUG SLOWED DOWN and peered curiously at the old Smith homestead as they passed it on the way to the village next morning. It was a shabby, gray-shingled Colonial house, close to the road. Set farther back were a barn and stable and a smaller outbuilding. Behind them a tumbling stone wall fenced the buildings from the pastureland up the hill beyond. At either end of the wall was a huge and ancient maple tree.

"The Twin Maples," Helen said softly.

They saw Priscilla weeding in the vegetable garden. She was obviously tired of her task, for she was resting back on her heels just watching the sky.

Pug had a chance to get a good look at her now — something he hadn't been able to do during that wild chicken-chase in Smithville. His first impression had been that she was spindly like his sister. But while Priscilla looked fragile, she must be tough inside, he decided. Her dark-brown eyes stared straight at a fellow, and her mouth and chin looked as if they came out of the same chunk of granite as her grandfather's.

Pug was so absorbed in watching Priscilla and in noting what a tumbledown look Twin Maples had, that he did not see the tiger kitten who was stalking a butterfly in the garden. Then he heard Ricky's sharp, delighted bark.

The beagle had leaped over the low picket fence and made a dash for the kitten. She arched her back and spat; but then evidently thought it wiser to make for the big maple beside the house. Ricky was after her in a flash.

"Pug, call him quick," Helen cried.

Priscilla had risen to her feet in a lithe movement and was calling in soothing tones, "Tiger, don't be scared, Tiger."

"Ricky!" Pug yelled angrily. "Come here, Rick." He got off his bicycle and ran to collar his dog. He apologized to Priscilla.

But Priscilla looked close to tears. "Tiger'll never get down from that tree by herself. She's just a kitten."

"Where's your grandfather?" Pug asked. His eyes were measuring the distance between the tree and the house. He could see a way to get the kitten down if —

"He's fixing the fence on the back pasture," Priscilla told him.

"Can you let me out of that upstairs window?" Pug pointed with his free hand at the south gable above the side porch.

She looked back at the fields and woods behind the house.

"If you hurry."

"Helen," Pug called to his sister, "take Rick and go on to the village. I'll get there as fast as I can. Ricky, go! Go!"

He gave the dog a shove toward Helen. Ricky knew he was in disgrace, but he looked back hopefully. Pug's voice was stern as he repeated, "Go! Go, boy."

When they were on their way, Pug turned to follow Priscilla as she ran lightly up the stairs to the south gable.

"This is Grandpa's room," she said. "Do be careful. But hurry! I don't think I ought to let you do it. You might get hurt. But I guess Grandpa used to climb out that window. Poor Tiger."

"I'll get her," Pug promised.

He slipped through the window to the narrow ledge. From there it was not as much of a swing as he had feared to the branch he had chosen to bear his weight.

He called softly to the kitten, and was answered with a piteous "mew" from Tiger.

Talking quietly, Pug made his way toward the frightened cat and dragged her from the tree trunk. Sitting astride a limb, he tucked her inside his shirt.

She clung as frantically to his bare chest as she had to the bark of the tree. Pug was glad he had partially smothered an "ouch," for that moment a man's deep voice roared:

"Prissy, what in tarnation is going on there?"

"A dog was chasing Tiger."

"What dog? Sounded like that varmint hound again — that Dibble dog."

"The dog is gone, Grandpa. Everything is all right now."

From his uncomfortable position in the maple, Pug fervently hoped she was right. He shifted a bit so he could peer down through the leaves.

Mr. Smith was leaning on his cane with both hands, frowning at his granddaughter. She had taken his arm and was trying to lead him away from the maple.

Would the old man go, giving Pug time to get the kitten to the ground and escape on his bicycle without being seen? As long as there was a chance of it, Pug decided to stay where he was and keep quiet. Another encounter with Mr. Smith might make it almost impossible to get the Smiths and Dibbles together on friendly terms.

Tiger had settled down inside Pug's shirt for a moment. If she kept quiet, he thought, he might be able to keep his seat in the tree. He wished Mr. Smith would go, but the old man stood his ground as if he had put down roots.

"Priscilla, what is going on here?" he asked again. "Stop pulling me!"

"I just want you to come back to the kitchen and rest a minute, Grandpa. I'll make some fresh coffee. You look tired."

"If I'm tired, it's because of all these Dibble shenanigans. That was their dog I heard, wasn't it?"

"Well, yes. But whatever it was that made you dislike the Dibbles so much, Grandpa, it must have happened ages ago. You can't blame *these* Dibbles for it. I wish we could be friends with them," she said wistfully. "The girl looks as if she would be nice to know. And the boy —"

Grandpa Smith pounded the ground with his cane.

"That boy!" he shouted. "That boy is the spit 'n' image of Nathanael Dibble. And when you're friends is when they twist the heart out of you. Any Dibble that sets foot on this place will go out faster than he came in!"

At that moment Tiger scrambled from Pug's shirt and Pug made a grab for her. The kitten yowled.

"What in tarnation?" Mr. Smith looked up, shading his eyes with his hand.

"Tiger is still up there," Priscilla's voice was choked.

"Sounds like a full-grown Bengal."

He lowered his hand and turned suspicious eyes on his granddaughter.

"What're you up to, Priscilla?" he demanded. "It isn't like you to leave Tiger up a tree."

He turned away from her and then spied Pug's bicycle leaning against the fence.

"Whose is that?" he asked grimly.

Pug admired the way she lifted her chin, and said bravely, "The Allen boy is up there getting Tiger down. She wouldn't come by herself."

Grandpa Smith glared up at the tree. "Boy, come down," he ordered.

With Tiger again buttoned inside his shirt, Pug inched his way from limb to limb until he reached the lowest crotch of the tree.

"I think Tiger can drop from here without getting hurt," he said to Priscilla. "Can you catch her?"

Without a word she spread her skirt wide. Pug released the kitten who sailed to safety like a flying squirrel.

Then Pug let go of the lowest branch. The tree trunk was too large to circle with his arms, and he slid the rest of the way, scraping off buttons and skin.

"Now git!" said Mr. Smith ferociously. "Git, before I use my cane where it would do a Dibble the most good. And stay off my place."

Pug lost no time in going over the fence. As he pedaled away, Priscilla called tremulously, "Thank you ever so much. I'm sorry you got all skinned up and tore your shirt."

Pug fumed all the way to the village. Helen had bought the bread and was waiting for him with Ricky in front of the store.

"For goodness' sake!" she exclaimed as she joined him on her bicycle. "Do you ever look as if you'd dropped dead twice and been stepped on!"

Angrily Pug told her what had happened.

"I'd guess from what he said about friends twisting the heart out of you that he and the Dibbles had been specially good friends once," she said thoughtfully.

"That's a safe enough guess," Pug muttered.

"You look a fright, but let's go see Miss Woodman anyway. I found out where she lives."

Pug protested because of his appearance. But when Helen insisted that she was going, he followed. He was afraid that he might miss something if he let her go alone.

CHAPTER 5

Fair Night, 1900

THEY FOUND to their surprise that Miss Woodman's cottage on Skyline Road was just behind Dibble Hollow. They could have reached it on foot across their own hilly fields.

A small, round-cheeked woman with white hair and snapping black eyes answered Helen's timid knock.

"Well, what is it?" she asked in a voice so deep that they both jumped.

Helen was tongue-tied now that they were face to face with Miss Woodman. It was Pug who had to answer.

"I'm Elisha Nathanael Dibble Allen." He was proud

of the way the name rolled from his tongue. "And this is my sister Helen," he added. "We —"

She interrupted him. "My land! You'd hardly have to tell me who you are. The Angel Gabriel himself would pass you for young Nathanael Dibble. Come in. Come in."

They followed her through the sitting room and dining room to the kitchen.

"I've got cookies in the oven," she said over her shoulder. "Sit down while I take a look at them. Can't depend on these newfangled 'lectric stoves the way you could on the old wood stoves."

She pointed to a couple of kitchen chairs at a table on which the cloth had been folded back half way. Rows of fragrant cookies were cooling there on a clean tea towel.

"Sit down and have a cooky," she invited. "Maybe you young ones nowadays don't like molasses cookies, but I get hungry for them every once in a while and bake me a jar full."

When Pug had bitten into the wafer-thin brown cooky, he declared in no uncertain terms that he liked them too.

Miss Woodman took a batch of cookies out of the oven and put in another.

"Now then," she said, seating herself in the low rocker by the window. "You must have some reason for coming to visit an old woman you never met. What is it?"

Pug liked her directness. He answered in the same way.

"We want to know what happened to make the Smiths hate the Dibbles."

Before answering, Miss Woodman got up and transferred the cookies from the cooling tin to the tea towel on the table.

"I suppose it's only natural you should want to know," she said at last. "Miles Dibble and Eb Smith were thick as thieves — well, maybe that's an unfortunate choice of words as it turned out, but that's what they were. Very close friends, at old Number Four School. And they both had older brothers who were friends too. What split the families wide apart happened at fair time the fall I was thirteen years old. The Smiths and the Dibbles had made quite a bit of cash money at that fair — what with prize bulls and selling some mighty good livestock and having a couple of fast horses. Our fair always had some good racing. Anyway, it turned out that they trusted the older boys to take the money home. And the older boys paid Eb and Miles to do it for them so they could stay longer for some high jinks that evening."

Miss Woodman took a peek in the oven, while Pug and Helen waited breathlessly for her to go on.

"No one knows exactly what happened, of course. Eb said they were followed by a couple of those men who always hang around country fairs hoping to gull a few country bumpkins. Eb thinks they saw the money change hands from the big boys to the younger ones, and figured it would be like taking candy from a baby to get it. So Eb and Miles split up. Eb was to take the men on a wild-goose chase while Miles was to take the money home."

Pug's heart was pounding with excitement as he listened. He felt as if he were living the adventure with Miles and young Eb.

"To make a long story short, Eb says he threw them off the trail. But when he got home, there was no sign of Miles. When the grownups got back, there still was no Miles at either house — and no money either. So the Smiths accused Miles of running off with the money."

"That couldn't be true!" Pug exclaimed. "Mom says a Dibble's word has always been as good as his bond. She's always telling us to remember that and keep it so. Doesn't she, Helen?"

Helen nodded.

"Well, it wasn't all one-sided," Miss Woodman went on. "The Dibbles accused the Smiths of maybe even going so far as to do away with Miles to get the money from both families' fair profits."

"Wow! What a mess!"

"I can see how both families would feel," Helen said slowly.

"Eb didn't believe Miles ran off with the money," Miss Woodman continued. "Not at first, anyway. He thought Miles was playing a prank on him because — well, maybe because of me. And Miles loved a joke. You see, things might have been quite different if I hadn't had mumps at fair time that year. Eb had asked me to go with him. Miles didn't like the idea at all. A girl can usually tell."

Helen was immediately eager to know about that.

"I think it was because Miles liked me himself," Miss Woodman smiled at Helen. "A girl can usually tell about that too."

"How could you tell?" Helen leaned forward.

"Miles was always trying to trip me at the skating pond — and one day he borrowed my best eraser and shaved it all to bits. And he would tie my sash to the desk seat so when I got up, I couldn't go any place. He wouldn't have been caught dead writing me a note himself. But I know he snitched one or two that Eb tried to pass to me. He just did things a boy does at that age to show a girl he likes her especially."

"How fantastic!" Helen giggled. "But — well, yes, I guess I know what you mean."

"It's probably because you young people are here that I feel as if Miles was right in this kitchen today, close enough to touch," Miss Woodman went on, closing her eyes. "Dear me! The cookies!" She jumped up and went to the oven.

Pug saw that her chair continued to rock madly after she left it. "She's righter than she knows about Miles being here," he thought.

"Oh drat!" she exclaimed, as she took out a sheet of burned cookies. "Well, blame it on Miles. Or the memory of him." She laughed a little. "He did love to tease."

"What about the thieves the boys said followed them?" Pug asked, bringing her back to the subject that interested him most.

"What? Oh, they were never found. That was what finally convinced Eb that Miles might really have taken the money after all. Because Eb said it was Miles who felt that they were being followed. It was Miles who suggested that they split up. Afterwards Ed began to wonder whether there really had been anyone on their trail. Especially when Miles was not found either. Of course the Dibbles had a memorial service for Miles when it seemed he must be dead. They put a stone for him in the old South Cemetery. But they never did find his body." She paused and sighed. "Disappointment in someone you think a lot of can just curdle whatever milk of human kindness you have. And that's what happened to Eb Smith."

"I wish there was something we could do to convince him *we're* all right," Helen said plaintively. "I like Priscilla Smith and it would be so wonderful to have a friend just down the road a little way."

Miss Woodman was sympathetic. "Prissy is a nice young one," she admitted. "Eb loves her and wants her to be happy. Only he can't abide the name of Dibble now. He's just plain mulish about it." She looked out the window and Pug had the feeling that she was looking away back into her own life. "Just plain mulish," she repeated. "I put my oar in long ago," she went on, "trying to make Eb see that a person doesn't hurt anyone but himself by carrying a grudge so long. He might have figured it that way too if only he hadn't had such misfortunes — and one after the other!"

"Like what?"

"It might help you to understand. I think I'll tell you." Miss Woodman leaned back in her chair and began to rock gently. "Eb married a city girl who was out here visiting one summer. They had a son, but Eb's wife died young, and he brought up their boy single-handed. The son was a restless lad and as soon as he was old enough he ran off to the city. Later he married, but the year Priscilla was born he was killed in the Far East. Eb brought the mother and baby back to Twin Maples and took care of them. Then Priscilla's mother took sick, and after a long illness, she died. It left Eb with a lot of debts, and a small girl to bring up."

"Zowie! That's a lot of misfortunes all right!" Pug said. "But he could hardly blame it all on Miles."

"True enough as far as it goes. But I guess he can't forget about the money that was lost that night they were children. You see, Eb had to mortgage the place as much as it would stand to take care of his expenses. That money would almost save Twin Maples today. And he lays that at your family's door."

"I wish we were rich," Pug said gloomily. "I'd pay off that mortgage so fast it would make you blink."

"Eb would never accept a cent from anyone," Miss Woodman said positively. "He's as independent as a hog on ice. Unless it was his half of the money that he and Miles were guarding, he would be just stiff-necked enough to refuse help." She shook her head. "I'll never believe Miles ran away with that money, though. He was a terrible tease and a show-off, but I can't believe he would do that. Still, I don't think the Smiths ever got the money either."

Pug and Helen thanked her and promised to come again, as she invited them to do.

They were silent almost half the way home.

"You know I had the queerest feeling while she was telling us about Miles Dibble," Helen said finally. "Especially when she said he seemed close enough to touch. It was creepy!" She shook her head as if to rid it of such nonsense. "We ought to try to do something about that mortgage even if it wasn't our fault," she added firmly.

"You heard Miss Woodman. She said Mr. Smith is as independent as a hog on ice."

"Maybe so. But we just might think of something." She pedaled abreast of Pug and then coasted. "If we could just think up a way to scrape up some money, perhaps we could plant it somewhere for him to find."

Pug was only half listening to Helen. He was impatient to get the whole story straight from Miles.

Suppose Miles did not show up again!

CHAPTER 6

Miles' Story

BEDTIME SEEMED TO COME at a snail's pace that
evening. Pug did not want to go up to his room
earlier than usual, for he did not want to arouse anyone's curiosity. But he found it hard to settle down
and do anything downstairs. He was so restless that
his mother felt his forehead to see if he had a fever.

His father, too, looked at him over his glasses when
Pug rose as the clock struck nine, said good night, and
went upstairs. Pug shut his door quietly and listened
to make sure Helen had gone on to her own room.

Suddenly a cold breath blew on the back of his
neck. A deep voice imitating Eb Smith's said in his
ear, "Boy, come down!"

Pug whirled about.

Miles was sitting by the window in the rocker.

"Come down out of that tree, boy," he said again in a deep voice.

"Okay, have your fun," Pug said coldly. "And when you're through goofing off, I have a few questions to ask you."

"You are my brother Nathanael all over again," Miles laughed. "Why? How? When? A living question mark! But save your breath to cool your porridge. I knew you would hunt up Fanny Woodman and I can guess what you want to ask."

"You followed us over there," Pug accused him. "Her chair didn't rock like crazy all by itself."

"I was there for a minute or two," Miles confessed with a grin. "I knew you would go to see her. And she would tell all. Fanny always was a gabber."

"She certainly believed in you. She said she was sure you hadn't taken the money."

Miles looked shamefaced. "That was when I was sorry I rocked her chair and burned her old cookies," he admitted. "I couldn't resist it when she said I was sweet on her."

Pug was impatient. "Tell me, was there really someone following you and Eb Smith that night?"

"There certainly was. Eb thought he got them off on his trail. But they were too foxy for him. They doubled back and went after me."

"Then what?"

"I did not have much headstart but I thought I

could outwit them by crossing the river on the old wooden bridge."

"You mean that broken-down bridge that isn't used any more?"

"There was no other in our day. Eb and I played on that bridge plenty of times — but only in daylight. The night of the fair was black as pitch. I was barely ahead of the thieves when I got to the bridge. I doubled my pace — and missed my footing."

Pug gasped. "Wow! Did you drop all the way to the river on those rocks?"

Miles rubbed his head and nodded ruefully. "The next thing I knew, those two villains were bending over me and one of them said, 'He's done for all right. Is the money on him?' "

Miles laughed silently. "You should have heard them when they found nothing but a few pennies and the new mouth organ I had bought at the fair." He started to pull the old one from his pocket but Pug stopped him.

"Go on, Miles. Tell me what happened."

"I tricked them slick as a whistle on the money."

"How?"

Miles continued as if he had not heard the question.

"Then the other one said, 'He's as dead as a mackerel and you can bet your bottom dollar we will be suspected if we hang around here. I'm getting out.' "

Miles stopped, and his eyes clouded over.

"Go on," said Pug. "Go on with the rest of the story."

"Well, all right. But you must remember it is an

old story to me and a rather painful one." He sighed.
"First the villains shoved me out into the river current
so that my body would be carried out to sea. But it
got caught on a pier and was fished out by a Mr.
Miller down in Milltown. He had me buried just as if
I had been his own son."

His twangy voice had softened as he mentioned
Mr. Miller. All of him disappeared except his face.

"Miles, don't go! Don't go!" Pug cried.

"Who said I was going anywhere? It is just that I
feel so carried away at this point in the story."

Pug breathed a sigh of relief. "What happened
then?"

"I came back here. When I saw how much trouble
my disappearance had caused, I could not rest until
the Smiths and Dibbles were friends again."

"You and me both, Miles! But the money? You said
you tricked the crooks."

"So I had. I could make scarcely any speed in these
boots, with the weight of the gold on me. So I hid it."

"Hid it?" Pug was breathless. "Then all you have
to do is help me get the money back to Mr. Smith!
Then everything will be okay again between our
families."

"It is not so easy to make everything hunky-dory
as you suppose."

"Why not?"

Miles looked uncomfortable. "The fact of the matter
is that I can remember as plain as day what those

ruffians said and how they cussed when they threw down my new mouth organ. But I am not certain just where I hid the gold."

"Oh, no!"

"If you had had the living daylights knocked out of you, I daresay you would not remember any better than I do," Miles pointed out.

"But why didn't you get hold of Eb right then and there? Why didn't you show yourself to him just as you did to me? Maybe the two of you could have figured out where the money was!"

"Why? Why? Why? Because I am not able to appear to anyone but a Dibble under fifteen — with a kind of a simple mind, I might add — I should think you could remember that. I told you this once before."

"Yes, I do remember." Pug was contrite. "Just me and one other special person, you said." He went on hurriedly, afraid Miles had been offended and would suddenly disappear. "Can't you look the countryside over in daylight and let *me* know where to hunt for the money?"

"I've been looking Twin Maples over for sixty years and I am confused every time. Eb and I had an old secret hideout. I tried that first thing. But I could never really have gotten that far that night. The hideout is high up on the rock ledge." He hesitated. "I do seem to remember that I put the money sack in a tree. But my sense of direction was never good."

"In a tree. Oh, fine! There are only a million trees

on the Smith place." Pug groaned. "I don't see much hope of getting the Smiths and Dibbles together until you remember which tree."

Miles sighed. "You are my only hope, Nathanael. I have been waiting for you a long time."

Pug sighed, too. "Maybe I can come up with something. I'll work on it. But go on — tell me about the Milltown part of the story."

"Have you ever been to Milltown?"

"No."

"Has anyone of your family ever been there?"

"No."

"It is not too far to go on that newfangled bicycle of yours. I am buried in the Gore Cemetery. At the far corner from the gate is the Gideon Miller plot. Next to the fence is the grave where Mr. Miller had me buried. He buried me like his own son because the boy had been lost at sea and he hoped someone would do the same for him."

They were silent a moment.

"What I can't understand, Miles, is how Mr. Miller could have done that in a town within bicycling distance, and no word of it ever got back here to Twin Maples and Dibble Hollow. Then folks would have known what happened to you, if not to the money."

Miles had whipped out his mouth organ and was playing an eerie melody that made Pug's ears ache. He stopped long enough to look at Pug pityingly. "I said 'a rather simple mind,' did I not?" he murmured. "Did you ever stop to think what this country was like sixty years ago? Dirt roads, no automobiles, no telephones around here. Letters were slower than molasses in January. And no one but an Indian ever traveled the Tumbling River."

He knocked his mouth organ against the palm of his hand. His whole face lighted up with a grin. "There is a good joke on the family, though," he chuckled. "They actually had word of where I was buried — and they never knew it. No, don't ask me any more!"

He raised his mouth organ again, but thought better of it, and instead began to sing:

> *Oh, I was down to Old Milltown,*
> *'Twas just the other day.*
> *I saw the biggest ram, sir,*
> *That was ever fed on hay.*
> *And if you don't believe me,*
> *And if you think I'd lie,*
> *Just you go down to Old Milltown*
> *And see the same as I.*
>
> *The horns upon his head, sir,*
> *They reached up to the moon.*
> *Two butchers went up in January*
> *And didn't come down till June.*
> *And if you don't believe me,*
> *And if you think I'd lie,*
> *Just you go down to Old Milltown*
> *And see the same as I.*

> *The man that killed the ram, sir,*
> *Was drowned in all the blood.*
> *And fifteen thousand soldiers*
> *Were carried away in the flood.*
> *And if you don't believe me,*
> *And if you think I'd lie,*
> *Just go down to Old Milltown*
> *And see the same as I.*

"Where did you get that old weirdie?" Pug asked, laughing.

"Oh, my father used to sing it. It came out in the *Milltown News* when I was knee-high to a grasshopper."

Miles yawned; then suddenly he was gone. Pug had the queerest feeling that Miles disappeared into the cavern of his own mouth.

CHAPTER 7

Discoveries

"OLD MILLTOWN" was still ringing in Pug's head the next morning. He would certainly make that trip on his bicycle as soon as he could. But there were so many things he wanted to do. Like finding Miles' hideout. And checking the route of Miles' adventure.

There was one thing he could do quickly. Pug went to the old South Cemetery and hunted up the Dibble plot of ground. There he saw the small stone with Miles' name on it and the dates: April 2, 1887-August 15, 1900. He sat down beside Miles' grave to think.

Pug had not expected any trouble confirming Miss Woodman's story. Everyone in town knew about it.

But what about that night at the old bridge? No one knew about *that*. Could he possibly find anything at the bridge that would show Miles had gotten that far on the fateful night?

Sitting there in the shade beside Miles' grave, Pug went over the story again in his mind. What about the mouth organ Miles had bought at the fair? The thieves had thrown it down in disgust when they could not find the money. Would a thing like that last for sixty years through all kinds of weather?

Pug got his bicycle at the gate of the cemetery and pedaled down the back road to the river. Only a piling here and there still stood to show where the old wooden bridge had been.

Pug parked as close as he could to the water and climbed down among the huge rocks at the shoreline. All morning he clambered over the rocks, first on one side of the wrecked bridge, then on the other. He looked all along the shore. Finally he gave up the search and decided to cool his feet in the water before going home to lunch.

A broad split rock slanted down to the water's edge. It looked like a good place to sit. Pug took off his sneakers and socks. But when he stood to roll up his jeans, he accidentally knocked one sneaker into the crack of the rock. Uh-oh — hope I can reach it, Pug thought anxiously. Lying on his stomach, he began to fish for his shoe in the split in the rock. Suddenly his eye caught the glint of noonday sun on metal.

Pug reached down and, unbelievingly, he pulled up a weathered mouth organ. His fingers shook as he wiped it carefully. The wood had almost all rotted away, and the metal plates were rusted but intact. Trembling with excitement, Pug placed the mouth organ carefully inside his shirt.

It took him twice as long as usual to put on his socks and shoes. "Five thumbs on both hands, just when I'm in a hurry," he muttered.

Then he dashed to his bicycle and headed home.

In his room, Pug scrubbed away enough rust and dirt to see the letters M D scratched on one metal surface. The mouth organ had indeed belonged to Miles! I have to find a really safe place to keep it, Pug thought. Maybe he could tape it to the back of the pine chest. Helen would never try to move a big piece of furniture like that.

Pug took hold of the chest near the top, and pulled and pushed until it came away from the wall. In the process, a loose pine knot fell out of the back of the chest. When Pug started to replace the knot he saw that behind the hole was a solid panel made of unevenly joined pieces of wood.

His heart leaped. With eager fingers he pressed first one piece of the wood and then another. Nothing happened. Then he pulled down on the bottom piece. There was a definite click.

In great excitement, Pug moved around to the front of the chest. The smooth wood above the top drawer now jutted forward slightly! Carefully Pug pulled at it, not daring to believe his eyes. It was a secret drawer! And in the drawer lay an old copybook.

Pug picked up the book and opened it. Yes, it had belonged to Miles. There were not many entries. The first was dated May 15, 1900.

May 15, 1900—Eb and I found a jim-dandy hide-out today. Followed the crick through two pastures to Billy Goat Hill. Tore my pants on the second rail fence. Took Eb and me both to pile up four rocks on top of each other to mark the spot on the ledge. Swore we would keep it a secret.

May 17—Ma gave us her old dough table and a chest for the hide-out. Had to let them down into the cave with ropes. Eb got two chairs. Found some old pots and a couple of candlesticks Ma said we could have out of the attic.

May 20—Raining cats and dogs. Hide-out dry as a bone. Decided to use Ma's chest in the hide-out for all our private stuff.

May 31—Went swimming today and caught billy blue blazes from Ma. Met Eb at the hide-out after supper and he said he got it from his Ma too.

June 25—Late for supper. Lucky Eb and I found some strawberries. Best spot we ever had. Up on the hill, left of the apple tree. Pa would have tanned me if I had not had the berries for Ma to make him some jam.

July 1—Eb's calf looks better than mine, but I have almost six weeks before fair time to fatten mine.

July 15—Eb and I have worked out a code. Ezra has been after Ma about the stuff we took from the attic. Besides he makes fun of us. It will serve him right if he finds one of our notes and cannot make head or tail of it. Eb says I better write the key down so I will be able to read the notes myself because I have a memory like a sieve. Gave him a black eye to remember there is nothing wrong with my fists.

At the margin of this entry, Pug saw the figures:

$$\frac{26}{3} = 0$$

Under this was a string of letters:

G Y K Q U C C R M L D Y L L W K W Q C J D

He read on:

Aug. 10—I have fifty cents saved for the fair. Going to get me a mouth organ. Eb thinks I am crazy. Says I cannot play for sour apples anyway. He wants a jack knife.

Aug. 11—Had a fight with Eb today. Saw him pass a note to Fanny. Lot of good it will do her. I got hold of the note he sent her. It gave away the key to our secret code. Criminentlies! I was mad as a wet hen.

Aug. 12—Fanny has the mumps. Made up with Eb. We are going to the fair same as always. He said I could use his new jack knife to scratch my initials on my new mouth organ.

That was the last entry.

Pug closed the yellowed book and put it back in the shallow drawer. Zowie! A hideout and a code! Twenty-six over three equals zero — that must be the key to the code. Pug wrapped the mouth organ gently in a handkerchief and laid it beside the copybook. Then he closed the drawer, replaced the pine knot, and shoved the chest back to its original position. Even on close examination he would never have known the drawer was there. What a hiding place!

CHAPTER 8

"Pure Accident"

Pug was eager to hunt for the secret hideout that Miles had described. He planned to do it that very afternoon, but it began to rain. And it continued to rain heavily for a week. Pug was the only one of the Allens who did not mind the rain. He was busy working on Miles' code.

It can't be so doggone hard, he thought. I'm not going to admit that Miles was that much smarter than I am. But I sure don't have much to work on. Let's see. Twenty-six over three equals zero. Then

G Y K Q U C C R M L D Y L L W K W Q C J D

Pug tried a number of things, but didn't break the code.

On the third rainy morning, Pug was having a

doughnut and a glass of milk. His mother was washing the breakfast dishes. Mr. Allen wandered into the big kitchen.

"All year I'd have given anything for time to relax and do absolutely nothing," Mr. Allen said. "And now I find I don't know *how* to do nothing."

He walked over to the window and drummed on the pane as he looked at the drenched landscape. "I've read and reread all the books. Anyway I'm too restless to read anymore."

"Why don't you listen to the radio?"

"Nothing but tripe in the daytime."

Mrs. Allen laughed, but Pug thought she did not sound really amused. "Honestly, Jim, you're as hard to entertain as the children," she said. "You might start the annual paper you always write for the Pen and Camera Club. I should think this would be an ideal time to get your material in order."

"Don't think I haven't tried. Nothing comes. I can't get two consecutive sentences on paper." He sounded frustrated.

Mrs. Allen finished drying dishes in silence. Pug was increasingly uneasy. They might have a long siege of rain. What if his father really was unable to find anything he liked to do in bad weather? Pug could not remember ever seeing his father sit idle. He was always reading or writing or working in his darkroom developing pictures. Pictures! Of course!

"Gee whiz, Dad!" he burst out. "Why don't you

print the snaps you took when we first got here?"

"With what?" his father asked. "I didn't bring my equipment. No room."

"But I brought some of mine," Pug said. "My trays and developing tank and everything may not be as good as yours but they'd be better than nothing." He glanced sideways at his mother. "I just brought the bare necessities, Mom," he said defensively. "All I left out of my bag that you told me to put in were my raincoat and galoshes."

"So that's why you're not out puddling around," his mother commented, in a milder tone than Pug had expected.

Mr. Allen quit jingling the coins in his pocket and turned from the window. "Developing pictures might help me get that paper started. But I'd need a dark-room."

"Couldn't you use the cellar?"

"No running water." Mr. Allen dismissed the idea of the basement with a wave of the hand. "The dark-room should be near the kitchen or the bathroom."

"How about the pantry?" Pug asked.

"I don't want —" his mother began; then threw up her hands feebly. "All right. Use the pantry. I've just been using the kitchen end of it. You can put the things I use out here, and the rest of the hodgepodge can go down cellar, I suppose. That counter and the shelves at the far end look as if the pantry had been used as a catchall for years."

"It does look like a glory hole," Mr. Allen admitted, opening the door and looking in. "But we can fix that, Alice."

"Sure, Dad and I can build you a cupboard right here in the corner of the kitchen where it'll be convenient," Pug offered. He was relieved to hear the note of cheerfulness that had crept into his father's voice.

"You and your father?" Mrs. Allen hooted. "You're both long on theory and short on practice. Perhaps you haven't noticed that I'm the one who fixes the ironing cord or puts a new washer in the faucet."

"I can build you a cupboard if I put my mind to it," Mr. Allen said firmly.

Mrs. Allen shook her head. "Unless the cupboard came in a kit complete with a gremlin to put it together, I might just as well call a carpenter."

Mr. Allen grinned but did not answer. He was already sorting the pile of things to go down cellar.

An hour later, Mr. Allen came upstairs, dusty and rumpled, with a dilapidated brown book which he held reverently.

"Look at what I found by pure accident," he gloated. "Listen to this title: *The Farmers and Emigrants Complete Guide, or a Hand Book with Copious Hints, Recipes, and Tables Designed for the Farmer and Emigrant.*"

"It was behind a drawer," Pug told his mother. "The whole drawer came out on top of him. What shall I do with this, Dad?" he asked, holding up an old hip boot.

"What?" Mr. Allen looked up vaguely from the book. "Oh — wear it, Pug. Wear it," he said, and went on reading.

Pug took immediate advantage of the advice and the fact that his mother was pushing his father into the living room with his book.

"Ha! We call this the do-it-yourself age," Mr. Allen was saying. "What about our forefathers? Alice, I've got it. My Pen and Camera paper will be about —"

Pug hurried back into the pantry to find the mate to his hip boot. There was Miles sitting on the counter, swinging his feet and whistling.

"Where have you been all this time?" Pug wanted to know. "I thought you must be mad at me."

"No, I just could not bring myself to appear in this weather. It puts a fellow in the doldrums."

"That's for sure," Pug agreed. "I was scared to death Dad would want to go back to Fairtown because of it."

"You can thank me that you are not loaded into that vehicle you call a station wagon and rolling toward the city right now," Miles said smugly. "I am your father's 'pure accident.'"

"What do you mean?"

"I came today just to get your father set up for the summer with plans for Dibble Hollow. He is the kind that always has to be doing something. I will show you where there is wood in the barn for that cupboard he is going to make."

"He won't fool with anything like that now that he has a good book and is getting ready to write his paper."

"You are mistaken, Nathanael. When he reads the handbook, he will aspire to be a master cabinetmaker. What a time I had pushing that drawer out on him so he would find it." Miles put his hands to his head and swayed back and forth. "That book was my grandmother's prized possession. I hid it after she gave me one of those witch's concoctions for a stomachache. It raised a hullabaloo, I can tell you, when that book disappeared." Miles laughed. "I thought I would have to go up in smoke before you would think of the pantry and let that handbook come to light. I must say, you have the imagination of a real Dibble, Nathanael, even if you are a little slow at a cipher."

"How would you look going up in smoke?" Pug asked eagerly.

In answer, there was a flash of lightning a clap of thunder, and Miles disappeared leaving a thin wisp of smoke which rose and drifted out the crack at the top of the pantry window. Pug shivered with delight. Then he clopped to the kitchen door as fast as he could in the heavy rubber boots. "I'm going out to the barn till lunchtime," he announced.

"What happened to that darkroom cleanup?" his mother asked.

"I'll get back to it right after lunch."

She shook her head despairingly. "You and your father. All right. Go ahead. Maybe if you're both out from under foot I can figure what to do with this mess."

"Dad will build you that cupboard, Mom. You just wait."

"That's undoubtedly what I *will* do — wait."

But at noon Mr. Allen surprised her. "Our ancestors had to do everything for themselves," he said. "They weren't all craftsmen either. They had to learn the hard way."

"Not in the late 1800's," Mrs. Allen observed. "If they had money, they hired someone to get things done."

"If they had money. Otherwise they did it themselves. I can do anything a Dibble could do."

"I found some good wood out in the barn today," Pug offered. "It looked about right for that kitchen cupboard, Dad."

"Lead me to it," his father said as they rose from the table. "There seems to be a doubting Dibble around here that we have to convince."

Mr. Allen spent the whole afternoon making a drawing and doing the figuring for the cupboard.

Pug stopped worrying for the moment about staying the whole summer. He saw his mother's contented look when she heard Mr. Allen whistling over the cupboard plans.

CHAPTER 9

The Strawberry Patch

THE RAIN CONTINUED for several days, but no one seemed to mind now. Mr. Allen was really excited about the cupboard he was building. Pug thought that his father looked younger than he had all year.

Pug kept working at the code, but so far he hadn't cracked it. If only Miles would give him some clue!

Clue? Hey, wait a minute, Pug thought. Maybe Miles *had* given him a clue. What was it he'd said last time? Something about a cipher. Miles had said that Pug was "slow at a cipher." Pug had been so busy watching Miles go up in smoke that he hadn't paid much attention to that remark until now. Suddenly it seemed very important.

"Cipher, cipher," Pug mumbled softly. He looked it

up in the dictionary. "Well, well, well," he said aloud in triumph. "Now we are getting somewhere." Cipher meant zero. But it could also mean a code — or *the key to a code*! Slow at a cipher, was he? He'd show that ghost!

Eagerly Pug got to work. " 'Twenty-six over three equals a cipher,' " he muttered. "Cipher is the key to a code. So 'twenty-six over three' is the key. But what could it mean?"

"Twenty-six . . . twen — of course!" The letters in the alphabet! Words are made up of letters, and there are twenty-six letters in the alphabet! Hurriedly, Pug wrote them in order on a sheet of paper:

A B C D E F G H I J K L M N O P Q R S T U V W X Y Z

"Twenty-six over three," he muttered. "Now what does 'over three' mean?" Then he looked long at the letters Miles had written:

G Y K Q U C C R M L D Y L L W K W Q C J D

In this jumble he saw that there were two c's and two l's. Those pairs certainly meant something. They must stand for letters that could be written as doubles — tt maybe, or oo or something. Pug knew that e is the most commonly used letter of the alphabet, so he decided to begin by substituting ee for one of the doubles in Miles' message. But which double?

"Over three," Pug said again. "Three must refer to letters. Sure! The third letter of the alphabet. That's the place to start!"

So under the cc in Miles' message, Pug wrote ee. Now let's see, he thought. If Miles had used his letters in their proper order, then his d should equal f, his g should equal i, and so on. With much erasing, Pug finally worked out the code. It looked like this:

A B C D E F G H I J K L M N O P Q R S T U V W X Y Z

Y Z A B C D E F G H I J K L M N O P Q R S T U V W X

Quickly Pug translated the message:

G Y K Q U C C R M L D Y L L W K W Q C J D

meant

I A M S W E E T O N F A N N Y M Y S E L F

Pug whooped as he separated the letters: I am sweet on Fanny myself. O boy, wait till he saw Miles!

Then he sighed. A lot of good that message was in helping to find the lost money. He put the copybook and the solution to the code away in the secret drawer.

The next thing he had to do was look for Miles' hideout. Then he would make that trip to Milltown.

Two days later the sun came out. Pug came downstairs early that morning and announced that he and Ricky were going to explore the farm. His mother asked him to take Helen along.

"You have both been indoors so long," she said.

"Oh, for Pete's sake, Mom," Pug groaned. "She'll just be a drag." How could he explain that he wanted to look for a secret hideout?

"Pug Allen, if I wear my jeans I can go wherever you can and just as fast too," Helen said indignantly.

"I should think you'd like to have company," his mother said mildly.

"Rick is all the company I need."

"All right then, I'll just follow you if you don't want to talk."

"Oh, fine!" All Pug's exasperation went into those two words; he was annoyed because he had not seen Miles since that fleeting moment in the pantry and there were so many questions he had to ask. Yes, he wanted to brag a little, too, about finding the diary and the mouth organ.

And now he had to have Helen tagging along after him when he was so eager to look for the hideout. It was too much. "Oh, fine," he repeated.

Helen started to cry. "If I just had Priscilla or *some*body that didn't bite my head off all the time!"

"Pug, I don't think it would hurt you to take your sister," his mother reproached him.

"Okay, okay. Turn off the waterworks," Pug said ungraciously. He had suddenly remembered the strawberry patch mentioned in the diary. "I suppose we could go look for strawberries." He made it sound like martyrdom.

Helen, however, cheered up at once.

"I think I know a super-duper spot to pick them," Pug said.

He continued to act like a martyr as he took the two quart berry pails his mother handed him. He whistled for Ricky and started out with Helen skipping beside him. She did not speak until they were past the culvert over the brook. There Pug hesitated.

"I thought you knew a super-duper place," she taunted.

"I'm just getting my bearings," he stalled, trying to remember what Miles' diary had said.

He started at a fast pace up the hill with Helen panting behind him.

"Do you really know a good spot?" she asked when they stopped a moment to rest.

He shaded his eyes and pointed up at the lone apple tree silhouetted against the sky. "Up there," he said briefly, "to the left of that tree."

Helen paused to pick a daisy. "Doesn't it give you a kind of queer feeling to look out over these fields and know that even before Mom was born the Dibble and Smith kids went looking for wild berries the same as us?"

Pug nodded amiably. During the brisk, early morning walk through country he already loved, his resentment had vanished. "Yeah," he said. "I bet Miles and Eb knew all the best places."

They followed the stone wall that bordered the field and separated the Dibble land from Twin Maples.

Pug was about to turn left from the apple tree at the top of the hill, with Helen still at his heels, when he thought he heard something. He stopped to listen. Someone on the other side of the stone wall was sobbing. He would have run in the other direction, but

Helen grabbed his hand and pulled him toward the wall. There in the meadow lay Priscilla Smith, face down, crying bitterly.

She stiffened suddenly as she felt their presence. When she saw Pug and Helen she leaped to her feet, wiping her eyes with the back of her hand.

"Gee, Priscilla, what's the matter?" Pug muttered awkwardly. "Can we help in some way?"

She shook her head miserably. "It's Grandpa."

"Has he been mean to you? I'll—"

"Nothing like that. He's going to lose the farm if he can't pay the mortgage in August."

"Oh, no!" Helen cried.

"He has enough money to pay the interest and he thinks Mr. Pratt will take that and give him more time to pay the rest of what he owes. But I heard Mr. Pratt at the store today. He didn't know I was down cellar getting jar rings for Miss Woodman."

Her chin lifted and she went on indignantly, "I heard him say that our place is an eyesore. He wants to take it over and sell it off to city folks in lots. If Grandpa can't pay the whole mortgage, he intends to snap up Twin Maples."

Pug was at a loss for words. Even Helen was speechless.

"Just imagine!" Priscilla cried, with a sweep of her arm. "All this beautiful land marked off in little lots with houses all over everything. And it's all my fault," she wailed.

"How do you figure that, for Pete's sake?"

"Grandpa had to mortgage the farm because he needed so much money when I was little."

"But it doesn't make sense to figure things that way," Pug told her. "If you did, you'd say the Dibbles are really to blame."

Priscilla looked at him questioningly.

"Well, if your grandfather had the money that got lost the night he and Miles Dibble brought it home from the fair, he could almost pay the mortgage. Ask Miss Woodman if you don't believe me."

"That's right," Helen chimed in. "That Mr. Pratt must be a meanie," she went on. "The idea of taking a person's home away!"

As Pug saw Priscilla's chin begin to tremble again, he said hastily, "We came to pick strawberries. I guess you did too." He nodded at Priscilla's pail with its sprinkling of lush fruit in the bottom. "We can talk and pick berries at the same time. Come on with Helen and me."

"Yes, come on," Helen begged. "Pug says we'll find the best berries over here to the left of that tree."

Priscilla hesitated. "Grandpa says *this* side of the tree is the best spot on the farm for wild berries. The right side."

"You did say left of the tree, Pug, didn't you?" Helen asked.

"Anyone could make a mistake like that," Priscilla said kindly. "But take a look around and see for yourself where the berries are growing. On the right."

"Well, come on over anyway," said Pug.

Just wait till I see Miles, he thought. Left from the tree, my foot!

"I'm afraid that Grandpa would have a fit, but —" Priscilla hesitated, but only for a moment. "You don't know how much I've wanted to be friends," she confessed, scrambling over the stone wall. "It seems so silly to be mad about something that happened years ago."

Pug was glad she had dried her eyes and seemed to forget the mortgage for the present. But while the girls talked, he was thinking of what Mr. Pratt had said about Twin Maples.

An eyesore, Mr. Pratt had called the place. In a way he was right. Pug himself had noticed that the grass needed cutting and the walls and fences needed repairs. Pug considered himself something of an expert on such things, for that was the way he had earned his spending money in town.

He broke in on the girls' conversation to say as much.

"You know if the front of the place was cleaned up, Mr. Pratt wouldn't be able to say it was an eyesore. Then he would have no good reason to take the farm."

"I know. But since Grandpa had to let Jake Holcomb go, it's beyond his strength. Jake wanted to stay, but Grandpa wouldn't let him because he couldn't pay him any more."

"Is your grandfather a sound sleeper?" Pug asked.

"If snores count, he is," Priscilla laughed.

Pug said no more, but while the girls chattered on,

he planned a little night work at Twin Maples. This would be a good night to start. The moon would be almost full. With moonlight, and his good auto flashlight, he would be able to see almost as well as in daytime.

At the dinner table that night Helen could talk of nothing but Priscilla and how cruel Mr. Pratt was to foreclose on Twin Maples.

"Oh, for crying out loud, Helen!" Pug exclaimed at last. "As Dad says, you can't foreclose until a mortgage is due. Plenty can happen before that. I'm going to bed. I'm practically dead tonight."

He left the room, yawning. Once upstairs, he checked the flashlight battery, and then slipped under the sheet with his clothes on. When the house was quiet and the hands on his clock told him it was eleven, he rolled out of bed, tiptoed to the window, slid one leg over the sill and located the ledge. With his flash slung around his neck on a strap, he had both hands free for the black cherry limb outside the window. Soon he was on the ground. He collected the gardening tools he had hidden under the front porch, and hurried off to Twin Maples.

There was Miles, sitting in the moonlight on the steps of Priscilla's house.

"That was real smart, Nathanael," he greeted Pug. "I mean your finding my new mouth organ the other day."

Pug was in no mood for compliments. "How did you know I'd be here?"

"Naturally I know all this village gossip about Zeke Pratt wanting Eb's farm. And I have my own way of knowing what you are up to. You know, you aren't bad for a city boy," Miles acknowledged. "I mean climbing down the tree tonight. Of course, Eb and I used to do a stunt like that in no time at all if we wanted to go fishing."

For a moment Pug's temper flared.

"Talk is cheap. If you're so great, why can't you remember where you hid the gold? I'm only fooling," he added quickly, as Miles suddenly looked hurt and started to disappear.

"I accept your apology." Miles resumed his seat on the doorstep. "And I am trying to find that hidden money. But there is no use digging up every tree on the farm. When I am sure which one it is I will tell you."

"Well, I hope you're surer than you were in your diary about the strawberry patch. Was my face red!"

Miles chuckled. "I am sorry about the strawberry patch. Eb used to say I never knew my right hand from my left. You were pretty luck to find my diary, Nathanael."

"I may have been lucky finding the diary," Pug retorted. "But you can't say that about the way I worked out your code. 'I am sweet on Fanny myself.' Ha!"

It was funny to see Miles blush. His whole face turned a queer red. "I never told her so. And I will thank you to forget it. I have put the whole thing out of my mind."

Pug laughed. "I'm not telling anyone, so don't worry."

"Oh to worry what's the use; better to be cheerful and spit tobacco juice," Miles changed the subject quickly.

"Cleaning up this place will help Eb a great deal, Nathanael."

Pug sighed. "Not enough. I'll have to get a better idea of it's going to take you all summer to remember where the money is."

"Yes, we both have to put our shoulder to the wheel," Miles admitted. "Think, Nathanael. Think like a Dibble."

CHAPTER 10

Pug Makes a Deal

P UG THOUGHT HARD about the best way to help the
Smiths. His big idea came a week later when he
dropped in at the village store for his mother.

"Makes me sick to see Twin Maples these days,"
Ezekiel Pratt was saying as Pug opened the door. "I
feel duty-bound to take over if Eb can't pay me my
money. The place is a disgrace to the whole valley."

Pug stood frozen.

"Too bad Eb had to let Jake Holcomb go," another
voice put in. "He was a good worker. An old man
needs help even on a small farm."

"Jake's making out all right. He's got the contract

for keeping up the green in Smithville. Ned Bailey
hires him all his spare time for his own place too."

"Well, now, I wasn't worrying about Jake," said
the other. "I was thinking of Eb and Priscilla."

"Nobody needs to worry about either of them,"
Mr. Pratt declared. "Mrs. Pratt and I will take Priscilla in like one of our own — and Eb won't have so
much to do. 'Sides that he'll have company his own
age at the County Home."

At that moment Mr. Hambly, the storekeeper, saw
Pug. The talking stopped. Pipes were knocked out
and matches were struck to relight them as Pug
walked to the counter and gave his order.

"Seen any ghosts?" one of the old men asked suddenly.

Pug hesitated — but only for a moment.

"Yes, I have," he said as casually as he could. "But
he's a Dibble ghost, so he's like one of the family."

The men chuckled appreciatively, as if they had
just heard a good joke.

Pug paid Mr. Hambly, picked up his parcel, and
then set it down again.

"May I leave this here for a while?" he asked. "I
think I'll bike over to Smithville before I go home."

"It's okay with me if your mother doesn't care,"
said the storekeeper. "Set it over by the window."

Pug thanked him. Then he turned toward Mr.
Pratt. At first he was afraid he was not going to be
able to say one word; his mouth felt so dry. He
knew he was blushing, too. Then he heard himself

saying, "Excuse me. I couldn't help overhearing you as I came in. Twin Maples is still Mr. Smith's farm, Mr. Pratt, and that is where he belongs. There have been Smiths at Twin Maples, I understand, as long as there have been Dibbles at Dibble Hollow — or before there were Pratts in Smithville," he added.

There was shocked silence for a moment.

Then Mr. Pratt said, in the kindly tone of one explaining something to a very small child, "Of course the Smiths have been there for years, my boy. But Eb Smith is too old to look after the farm any longer. And Priscilla is too young. Suppose one of them should take sick? He'll have good care in the County Home with regular meals, medicine, anything he needs."

"I don't see how you can even *think* of putting a man like him in a home."

"It would be for his own good." Mr. Pratt was still being reasonable.

"His own good! It would kill him. And don't be too sure he won't have the money to pay off his mortgage," Pug went on recklessly. "You can't touch him if he does that." He stopped for breath. "If Priscilla ever needs a place to live, I'm sure my mother and father would take her in with us. She won't be a babysitter with us either."

He was aware of assorted coughs as he went out quickly, letting the screen door slam behind him. He was trembling so that he could hardly pedal as he headed for Smithville. Maybe his father and mother would be angry when they heard what he had done. But how could he keep quiet?

Pug slowed down. What was he going to do now? A half-formed idea began to take shape in his mind. But first he had to look over Mr. Bailey's place in Smithville to see if his scheme would work.

The Bailey house was the third from the old Congregational Church facing the village green. Pug walked past it slowly, figuring out how much work it needed. Yes, this would be a job he could handle.

Back toward Bank Street he went now, determined to see Mr. Bailey, president of the Citizens' Bank. He walked past the bank three times before he worked up enough courage to enter. Then he plunged through the door and walked up to the desk which said "New Accounts."

"I'd like to see Mr. Bailey, please," he told the fairhaired young man who looked up inquiringly.

The clerk eyed him appraisingly.

"It's a private matter," Pug said.

"Perhaps I can help you. Mr. Bailey is very busy."

Pug shook his head. "I'd like to see Mr. Bailey."

The clerk still hesistated, but with another look at Pug's tense face, he said, "Who shall I say is asking for him?"

"Elisha Nathanael Dibble Allen." Pug accented Nathanael.

The man blinked twice and coughed suddenly.

"Of Dibble Hollow," Pug added efficiently.

The young man nodded and left quickly. He reappeared a moment later with a tall, bald-headed man, whose gray eyes looked Pug over sharply. Then he said, "Come in, Elisha *Nathanael* Dibble Allen. Come in."

He held open the door marked "Private" and closed it behind Pug.

Mr. Bailey waved Pug to a seat. He then sat down at his desk in a creaking swivel chair and tilted it back.

"You wanted to see me?"

"Yes, sir. I heard today that you hire Jacob Holcomb for your yard work."

"That's so."

"I went past your house a few minutes ago, and I'm sure I could do the same kind of job as Mr. Holcomb does for you."

"Perhaps. Only I don't need two men and I couldn't let Mr. Holcomb go. That would hardly be fair."

"No, sir. I wouldn't ask you to let him go — only just lend him while I do his work at your place."

"Lend him?"

"Yes — to Mr. Smith out at Twin Maples."

"To Eb Smith?" Mr. Bailey came forward in his swivel chair and leaned on his desk. "Didn't you say your name was Dibble?"

"Yes, it is." Pug was defiant. "And I've heard about the trouble between the Smiths and Dibbles till I'm fed up. It doesn't make sense."

"Granted. But the grudge is very real to Eb Smith. He has lived with the idea since he was a boy."

"That's why I thought maybe you could pay Mr. Holcomb to go out and help Mr. Smith — an under-cover job, you know — and Mr. Smith would just think Mr. Holcomb was giving him a helping hand. From what Priscilla says, he and Mr. Holcomb get on fine. and he might take the work as friendly help — you know, the way they used to get together to raise a barn or something in the old days. The way it says they did in the *Emigrant and Farmers Hand Book.*"

Mr. Bailey's big square hand drummed on the desk as Pug paused for breath.

"I don't know why I didn't think of something like that myself," he said slowly. "But —"

"I would do Mr. Holcomb's work for you for nothing," Pug put in quickly as Mr. Bailey's brows drew together in a frown. "I figure I could do your lawn in one day, once a week. I'm very experienced, you know."

"Are you, now? Well, well. This does beat the Dutch."

Pug thought Mr. Bailey would stare a hole through him.

"And what do *you* get out of it?" Mr. Bailey asked at last.

"Nothing except we're trying to get Twin Maples spruced up so Mr. Pratt can't say Mr. Smith isn't able to look after it any more. Only Mr. Smith won't let me set foot on Twin Maples, and —"

Mr. Bailey scratched his bald head. He swiveled in his chair twice. Then he got up abruptly. "I don't know of anyone who can get around Eb Smith the way Jake Holcomb can," he said. "I'll tell him he's free on Fridays to work at Twin Maples and he won't lose by it."

"One thing has to be sure and certain," Pug said.

"What is that?"

"Nobody must know about this. They talk too much around this town."

Mr. Bailey grunted. "That's as sure as you're born, Elisha Nathanael Dibble Allen. Is it Nathanael, for short?" he asked.

"Yes, sir."

"Well, Nathanael, if no one knows about this but you and me, you won't get a mite of credit."

"That suits me," Pug nodded his satisfaction. "If we can just straighten out the trouble between Smiths and Dibbles we might get my dad to stay on here for good, instead of just for the summers." Pug was expressing his own wistful dream. "But Dad can't stand the bickering and quarrels." He sighed.

"Your father is a teacher, isn't he?"

"Yes, sir. He's probably the best teacher in the whole United States."

"I shouldn't doubt that for a minute," Mr. Bailey agreed heartily. "Where does he teach?"

"Paxton High in Fairtown where we come from."

"I expect they'd give him quite a recommendation, wouldn't they?" He patted Pug on the back as he escorted him to the door.

"Nathanael Allen is to be admitted whenever he asks for me," he told the goggle-eyed clerk.

Pug was gleeful as he pedaled homeward. I won't be doing any more work than if I did it at Mr. Smith's, he thought. And I won't have to work nights. I can do it in the daytime.

He stopped at the store to pick up his bag of groceries and was glad no one was there but Mr. Hambly. Pug was dumbfounded when the storekeeper handed him a small bag with his other package.

"Thought you and your sister might have a sweet tooth," he said casually. "My kids like peppermints.

"Think nothing of it," he mumbled when Pug thanked him. He checked off an item on the order he was filling. "Some of us around here think a heap of Eb Smith, ornery as he is," he commented without looking up. "It's good to hear a Dibble understand him and know Eb's bark is a whole lot worse'n his bite."

Pug was still sucking one of the peppermints when he pedaled slowly past Twin Maples. He could already imagine the difference Jake Holcomb would be able to make in its appearance. His mind went back to Mr. Bailey and Mr. Hambly.

The people around here are the kind I'd like for friends, he thought. I wish we could live here all the time. The summer is going too fast. Much too fast, especially if he was to keep Mr. Pratt from taking over Twin Maples. He wondered again uneasily what his parents would say if they ever learned what happened today at the store.

He found out a few days later when his father said gravely at the lunch table, "I was sorry to hear at the store today that you were rude to Mr. Pratt, Pug."

"Who? Me? I never said anything rude to him. What was it?"

"It seems you practically told him he had no right to take possession of Twin Maples if Mr. Smith could not pay the mortgage when it's due. And you rebuked him for thinking Mr. Smith would be better off at the County Home than alone and unable to care for the farm and his granddaughter."

"Well, no one else said anything when he said that's where Mr. Smith ought to be. And you know it would kill him, Dad — an independent old man like him. Besides, all I said was that it was still Mr. Smith's farm and not to be too sure of taking it over because Mr. Smith might have the money to pay him."

His father went on as if he did not hear.

"You also implied, I gathered, that if the Pratts gave Priscilla a home it would amount to a baby-sitting job."

"Well it would," Helen cut in. She had been listening wide-eyed to the conversation. "The Pratts have four children younger than Prissy," she went on rapidly. "And they can't keep anybody to help them because the children are such — such a headache."

"Calm down, Helen, until I see this through," Mr. Allen said quietly.

"They also told me that you were asked if you had seen any ghosts since coming here," he went on, turning again to Pug. "And that you said you had, but it was a Dibble ghost so it was like one of the family."

Pug squirmed. "Well, yes. I guess that's about what I said all right. They thought it was kind of funny."

"Do you think that kind of joke is going to help the reputation this house already has?"

Pug held his breath as his father looked first at him and then at his mother.

He began to breathe again when his mother laughed outright.

"Oh, Jim. Ask a silly question, and you get a silly answer. Ghosts! What nonsense!"

Mr. Allen nodded. "All right, Pug. I just don't want you to be disrespectful to anyone. Mr. Hambly did seem to feel that it wouldn't hurt Mr. Pratt to realize Twin Maples is not actually his yet."

"It is serious, though, Dad. And maybe I ought to tell you I've made sort of a deal that I hope will help Mr. Smith a little." He looked sideways at Helen and back to his father. "I'd just as soon not say exactly what — but it's honest. I just have to be away from home a day or two a week."

"Perhaps you'd better give me a few details." Mr. Allen, too, looked at Helen. "Later."

"Don't worry about leaving me out," she said virtuously. "I'm not interested in what Pug does to help the Smiths. Priscilla and I have a plan or two of our own, you know. But if you know any secrets about Dibble Hollow, Pug Allen, and aren't telling me, I'll — I'll *haunt* you."

"Now what could I know that you don't?" Pug asked wide-eyed.

"Plenty! The way you go pussyfooting around. Locking doors and everything."

"Well, for Pete's sake, a person has to have a little privacy once in a while."

"All right, that's enough." It was Mrs. Allen's no-nonsense voice.

"I just want him to know Prissy and I have something to do tomorrow and he'd better not follow us."

"That's A-OK with me. Where are you going?"

"Wouldn't you like to know?"

"Just so I can go in the other direction."

"Pug! Helen! I said that's *enough!*" Mrs. Allen said sternly.

Pug was secretly glad to know Helen would be busy the next day. It would give him the free day he needed to make that trip to Milltown.

CHAPTER 11

Milltown

LATER THAT EVENING Pug told his father about his deal with Mr. Bailey. He also asked permission to take a bicycle trip the next day. "I'd like to do some exploring around here when I don't have to take Helen along," he explained.

His mother was hesitant. But Mr. Allen said, "I think we should let him go, Alice. Pug knows the traffic rules and he's usually pretty responsible. Remember he's been on overnight bicycle trips with the Scouts."

That settled it. His mother agreed. "I want to know where you're going, though, Pug."

"I figured I'd head toward the coast — toward Milltown. It's not very far and I could take the river road. There wouldn't be so much traffic on it, and if I follow the river there isn't a chance in a million that I'd get lost."

"I'm not exactly afraid of your getting lost as long as you have eyes and a tongue in your head," Mrs. Allen told him as she packed his lunch box. "And I guess your father is right — you are used to traffic and you do know the rules. But you will be careful, won't you, dear?"

Pug set out that morning with a light heart, a full lunch box, and enough money to phone home if he ran into any trouble.

It was a perfect July day. The sun was hot. The river road was shady. Pug felt wonderful. By mid-morning he reached the main highway. An hour later he was on the outskirts of Milltown. He spotted the wrought-iron gateway of Gore Cemetery before he actually got into the city.

"At one of the far corners from the gate there's a plot in the name of Gideon Miller," Pug repeated softly to himself. "That's what I'm after."

He rode through the arched gate and round the fence to the back of the cemetery. At the far right corner in a fenced-off area he read the name "Miller" on the largest of several headstones.

Pug got off his bicycle and began to read the names on all the stones. There it was — the one he was looking for! A stone in the corner bore the name of

"Gideon Miller, Jr. — August, 1900." Below the name there were several lines of engraving.

Haltingly he whispered the words:

My son, poor lad, was drowned at sea;
So was his body lost to me.
This body here with name unknown,
Shall have the honor of my own.
And so may both, O God, in Thee
Find rest through all eternity.

Pug's whisper trailed off. He stared in silence.

The Millers must be important people around here, he thought. I don't know if I've got the nerve to find out if some of them still live here. But as long as I'm here, I'd be foolish not to try. Maybe they'd know about the family at the courthouse in Milltown.

He rode slowly out to the gateway. Glancing left and right for oncoming traffic, Pug saw a gate across the highway. On the gate was the inscription "Gideon Miller School for Boys."

Say, that would be a good place to ask questions, Pug thought.

It turned out to be even better than he had hoped. The headmaster of the school, Mr. Dobbs, treated Pug like an adult when he told him who he was and that his father was a teacher too. He did not seem to find it strange that Pug was interested in the tombstone of Gideon Miller, Jr.

"That story is well known here in the school," he said. "Mr. Miller was a very young man then. His only son had gone to sea as a cabin boy and was lost in a shipwreck. After that, Mr. Miller used to spend considerable time down at the wharves. One day he found a drowned boy there whose clothes were caught on one of the pilings. He pulled him out and had him buried in the family plot as if he were his own son."

"He never found out who the boy was?"

"Not to my knowledge."

"I don't suppose Gideon Miller, Sr., is still alive?" Pug asked hopefully.

"Oh, but he is. In fact we are preparing a celebration in honor of his ninety-fifth birthday."

"He lives here?"

"At the big stone house next door."

"Do you think I could see him?"

The headmaster shook his head decidedly. "I'm afraid not. The old gentleman is very frail. He's saving all his strength for this affair on his birthday. I think it would upset him greatly to talk about something he still seems to feel keenly. He's quite — fanciful at times. Nothing serious, you know. But he talks to himself a bit — or to his lost son. He could not tell you more than I have already told you — anything sensible, at least."

Pug thanked the headmaster and went back to his bicycle. But he was not quite satisfied. He looked longingly at the square stone house a short distance from the school. Maybe something *could* be learned from Mr. Miller even at this late date. Mr. Dobbs

had described him as a fanciful old man who talked to himself or to his lost son.

A thought popped into Pug's head. What if —? "Wow! I wonder," he said out loud, with mounting excitement.

Pug bicycled down the service road to the next gate.

The elderly man who answered his knock at the stone house was kindly but firm in refusing to allow him to see Mr. Miller.

"He never sees anyone but family," he stated positively and started to shut the door.

"Will you just ask him if he will see a friend of Miles?" Pug begged. "I mean just *ask* him. If he says no — then all right. I'll go away. But won't you ask him?"

"Just a minute then." The man shut the door.

He was back much sooner than Pug expected, looking quite mystified.

"Come in," he said. "Mr. Miller will see you."

Pug followed him across a central foyer into a huge room. It was furnished with massive mahogany pieces. On the fireplace mantel was the model of a full-rigged sailing ship. Pug glimpsed it fleetingly, then his whole attention riveted on the old, old man sitting in a morris chair by the window. Pug had never seen such a finely wrinkled face as Mr. Miller turned toward him. Nor such startlingly clear blue eyes. A fringe of wispy white hair circled the shiny bald crown of his head.

Without taking his eyes from Pug, he said, "Ye can go, Ben." His voice was surprisingly strong, with a blend of New England and Scotland in its inflection.

"Well, laddie," he said, when Ben had reluctantly closed the door behind him.

"I am Elisha Nathanael Dibble Allen from Dibble Hollow," Pug introduced himself. "I'm a friend of Miles —"

"Miles? Miles who?"

"Miles Dibble, Mr. Miller. The boy you buried as you would have your own son."

"A friend of his you say? That lad died sixty years ago."

"Yes, I know."

"It makes ye a bit older than ye look — or —"

"You did find out who he was, Mr. Miller," Pug accused him gently.

"Aye, laddie, that I did," he acknowledged finally. "But not until a year later, and not through the usual channels."

He sucked in his withered cheeks. "Not the usual channels," he repeated. "It was when I was very ill, ye understand — delirious."

Pug nodded. "He came and sat on your bed?"

Mr. Miller looked at him intently.

"Aye," he said at last.

"How did he look?"

"Just as he did when I fished him out of the water, but dry of course." With eyes screwed shut, he described Miles.

Pug nodded again.

"I thought it was just delirium," Mr. Miller continued. "But I begged him to come again anyway. And he did. He said he owed it to me."

He darted a look at the closed door and put a long bony finger to his lips.

"In a practical world 'tis best not to mention seeing what no one else sees," he suggested with a slight roll of his r's. He leaned forward, his blue-veined hands on his knees, and said in a lowered voice, "I would not have my will contested on the charge that I am daft, do y'see? So I have not mentioned our friend to anyone — ever. Nor ever will."

"So you are the one special person who can see Miles," Pug said softly. "I am the other one — because I am a Dibble boy, you see, and under fifteen. I came to see you because I thought Miles might have said something to you, while it was fresh in his memory, about what he did with the money he was guarding the night he died."

Mr. Miller shook his head regretfully. "Nary a word. Knocked clean out of his head, I shouldn't wonder. And he would never take a cent from me. Said his spirit would never rest until the buried money was found. I urged him to keep trying until he had a Dibble to help him. With you to prod and encourage him, he'll recall it, I've no doubt."

"It's the shortage of time that bothers me," Pug sighed.

"Aye, laddie. Aye. Shortage of time it is."

Mr. Miller sank back in the chair and leaned his head against the cushion. In repose he looked deathly tired. With a sudden twinge of conscience, Pug rose from the hassock to which Mr. Miller had motioned him when he came in.

"Thank you for seeing me, Mr. Miller," he said. The old man roused himself to say good-bye.

"Mum's the word," he whispered, and rang for Ben to let Pug out.

Though he had learned nothing about the whereabouts of the hidden money, Pug was glad he had had a chance to see the man who had befriended Miles, the only other person to whom Miles could appear.

The trip home seemed long and tiring. But he was there before dinner time. He came into the kitchen as Helen was speaking, in her usual dramatic way.

"What do you think I heard today? They need a new math teacher at Smithville High School this fall, Daddy. Couldn't we stay on and you teach there?"

Mr. Allen shook his head. "There's too much tension here, belonging to a feuding family, Helen — even if they wanted me to teach."

"Jeepers, Dad," Pug said, setting his lunch box on the table. "It seems to me you were always under some tension or other back in Fairtown, what with town politics and everything. If the Dibble-Smith feud were cleared up, could we stay then?" He was as eager as Helen.

"Where would I get in the teaching profession, buried here in the country?"

Mrs. Allen had been quietly shelling peas. After Mr. Allen's last remark, she said thoughtfully, "It seems to me we already are someplace. We wouldn't have to get anywhere. We could put down roots and have a real home." She paused. "But only if you felt that way about it too, Jim."

"The villagers think of us as summer people, you know."

"That's what we are at the moment. But if we stayed on — after all, my family lived here for generations." She hesitated again. "I thought when you built my kitchen cupboard and fixed the back steps, that you were really beginning to get the feel of the old homestead."

"Perhaps I am. It has been a challenge to match my skill with that of another generation. And I like these present-day villagers too. But whether I could stand living at Dibble Hollow with the past constantly rearing its ugly head — I don't know." He said it jokingly but Pug knew he more than half meant it.

"I've got some ideas on that, Dad. If we did get the past straightened out, would you stay?"

Mr. Allen looked from Pug to Helen.

"My, you two seem set on it. Yes, I might consider it," he said.

Helen sighed. "About the only way you could fix up the past is suddenly come up with the money Miles had on fair night and pay off the Smith mortgage," she declared.

Helen wasn't so dumb, Pug decided.

"Or else raise the money some other way," she added slyly. "Is that what you're doing on Fridays, Pug?" she asked in her sweetest voice.

"What I'm doing isn't something you could help with," he told her coldly.

He was sorry the minute he said it. It was a sure challenge to Helen to find out what he was doing.

But Helen only smiled. "Who said I wanted to help? Priscilla and I are busy with plans of our own."

CHAPTER 12

Encounter with the Pratts

PUG WANTED TO TALK to Miles that same night about his bicycle trip to Milltown. So he was sorely disappointed that Miles did not appear all that week. Pug finally decided it must be because Helen stuck so close to him trying to discover what he was up to.

"Honestly, she's just like a leech, Mom," he complained.

It was Thursday evening. The family had gathered in the kitchen to crack and shell nuts for the cake Mrs. Allen had promised to make for the church social. It was being held in Smithville the next day.

"She just can't come with me tomorrow to Smithville because I'll be too busy to look after her," Pug explained.

"Is that so!" said Helen. "Well, it might interest you to know, Mr. Important, that I couldn't go with you if you begged me on bended knee. I'll be busy myself."

Pug looked at her suspiciously. She had not used the hurt tone she usually assumed.

"It's a good thing," he commented. "Because my business won't stand for females hanging around."

"Helen is going to help me make the cake. So you can put your mind at rest, Pug."

"His so-called mind," Helen amended. "But the cake won't take all day, Mother. And I do have some other plans too."

"I'll bet you do." Pug was sarcastic. "And they'd better not include me."

"Some people don't sit around all summer long waiting for mortgage money to grow on trees — or looking for lost treasure," Helen said, eating the nuts she had just picked from the shell.

Pug had placed a nut on the flatiron between his knees and was about to crack it with the hammer. But at Helen's words he laid the hammer down and said vehemently, "Look, I'm not exactly sitting around. And what I'm doing will beat any of your half-baked schemes."

"Any half-baked scheme I have will be as good as yours, so there!" Helen flared back at him.

"Gee whiz, Mom, she'll ruin everything."

"I don't think so, Pug. We're trusting you and Mr. Bailey on your business deal. Helen has told me her plan and you should trust us not to let her do anything to interfere with yours."

"Okay. But she'd better stay out of my hair."

"Don't worry. We won't bother you," Helen said sweetly.

"What do you mean, 'we'? "

"Prissy and I, of course. I should think even you would admit she has a right to try to do something to save the farm and her grandfather and herself from — from a fate worse than death!"

He had to admit that. And his mother had practically guaranteed to keep the girls out of his way in Smithville too. Now maybe he would get to see Miles again.

Even though he had been on the lookout for Miles, Pug almost bicycled off the road the next morning when the familiar voice said in his ear, "Sorry I can't help you pedal up this hill. The spirit is willing, but the flesh is weak." Miles chuckled loudly at his joke.

Pug turned his head enough to know Miles was riding the luggage carrier behind him.

"Holy smoke! Do you have to scare a fellow to death? And where have you been? I was afraid you weren't coming back."

"No. I cannot give up until I finish the task," Miles sighed.

"Well, we haven't much time before that mortgage

is due," Pug said anxiously. "And what's more, the girls are out on a 'save the farm' program now and there's no telling what they've cooked up."

"They cannot upset the applecart. Let them go ahead. It will give them something besides boys and baubles to think about."

"Helen's smart," Pug protested. "I wouldn't be surprised if she had a good plan. She's as anxious to be friends with Priscilla as you are to fix things up with Eb Smith."

"I do not underestimate Helen," said Miles. "She and Priscilla are all right as girls go. Better than most. I could tell them where to find a couple of things they would give their eyeteeth for."

"You know what they're up to?"

"I can guess. They have been over to see Fanny Woodman a couple of times."

Before Pug had time to ask Miles *why* Helen had been seeing Miss Woodman, his free-loading passenger asked, "Have you found our hideout yet?"

Miles' hideout was one of the places Pug had wanted to find almost as much as he wanted to located that hidden gold.

"Not yet I haven't," said Pug. "But I haven't had time enough to really look. If you'd give a guy a clue —"

"*Take* time for the hideout," Miles urged. "I cannot tell you any more than I said in my diary. But what a hideout it was! And what a job Eb and I had getting Ma's dough table and her little chest down in there! Hunt up a friend. When you find the hideout you will need him."

They were coasting down the last long hill into Smithville and Pug had to keep his mind on what he was doing. By the time he pedaled into town, Miles was gone.

Preparations were being made for the lawn social and cake sale as he passed the church. There was that boy — Ernie Pratt, Mr. Pratt's son. He was nailing strips of colored crepe paper on a table with sawhorse legs. He was doing a good job and seemed to be enjoying himself.

Ernie looked up and saw Pug. For a split second it looked as if he would speak. Pug thought afterward it might have been his own grim expression that stopped Ernie. Pug was thinking of the chicken episode on the day they arrived in Smithville. Ernie lowered his head and went back to his table-trimming, paying elaborate attention to the way he placed the colored strips. Pug watched a minute, and then rode on to Mr. Bailey's.

He began working at once on Mr. Bailey's place. Before doing any mowing, Pug gathered up the apples that had fallen. He had just set out the bushel of fallen fruit and was starting to gather up the twigs and stones that could wreck the mower, when Ernie came walking by the fence, wheeling his bicycle.

"Where's Jake Holcomb?" Ernie asked abruptly.

"It's his day off," Pug replied.

"What are you doing here?"

"I'm a spaceman looking for uranium." Pug affected a clicking sound like a geiger-counter.

"Wise guy, huh?"

"Well, ask a stupid question and you get a stupid answer. Hey — watch out for those apples in there!" Pug said sharply, as Ernie leaned his bicycle against the basket.

"Why should I? They're on village property. I can put my bike against them if I want to and nobody can stop me."

"Is that so?"

"Yes, that's so. They're not inside Mr. Bailey's fence. I can do anything to them I want to."

"You'd just better not touch them, or I'll —" Pug threatened.

"You'll what?" Ernie grinned provocatively. Then he leaned down and turned the basket over. Pug would have rushed out to settle things with Ernie then and there, but at that moment Mrs. Bailey came out on the back porch with a plate of cookies and a jug of lemonade. Ernie got on his bicycle and nonchalantly rode away.

Pug was boiling — with anger and from the heat of the day. He was very grateful for the refreshments.

"I'm going over to the church with cookies and a cake now," Mrs. Bailey informed him. "If Prissy Smith should come while I'm gone, ask her to wait, will you, Pug? I want to talk to her before —"

Her voice was drowned out by the yelling of children coming down the walk. Mrs. Bailey shook her head as she watched them.

"Those youngest Pratt children," she murmured when the noise had abated. "Just like yeast in a bowl of dough. They can raise more cain than — than Adam and Eve could." She looked rather shamefaced. "A saying of Mr. Bailey's," she explained. "I really shouldn't say it. But it does seem as if we don't have a peaceable social unless the Pratts are home with mumps or measles or something."

"I know what you mean," Pug said ruefully. "I just had a run-in with Ernie."

"The funny thing is that Ernie is not really a Pratt," said Mrs. Bailey. "He was only two years old and his mother was a widow when Zeke Pratt married her. Then Ernie's mother died, and Zeke married again. I'll say this for Zeke — he has always treated Ernie like his own. Ernie's stepmother, though — well she's a mite partial to her own children and pays no attention to Ernie most of the time. How ever did I get off on that tack? Oh, yes. What I started to say is that I want to see Prissy when she brings the eggs."

Pug thanked her for the refreshments and promised to tell Priscilla. "Gee, Mrs. Bailey, I didn't know she was bringing your eggs today. I could have carried them over for her."

"That's neighborly of you, Pug, but it makes a

little change for her to get over here on an errand. I won't be away long."

Pug put his plate of cookies on top of the hedge and the jug of lemonade under it. Then he pulled up the apple basket Ernie had tipped over. Maybe Ernie had been right in saying the apples were on village property. But he didn't have to push them over. Even as he muttered about it, Pug knew that he had practically dared the other boy to do it.

He had just finished his second cooky when he saw Priscilla at the gate, carrying the basket of eggs. Helen was with her.

"So this was your big deal!"

Helen and Pug said it in the same breath; then they both laughed.

"I don't know why you had to be so mysterious about doing some yard work," Helen said, recovering first.

"Same reason you had to be so hush-hush about bringing over some eggs for Mrs. Bailey," Pug retorted. "And I don't see how it'll raise enough money for the mortgage to sell eggs."

"Maybe it's not just eggs. We —" Helen broke off as Mrs. Bailey appeared.

"Good morning, girls. Come right in. You must be ready for some lemonade too."

It seemed to Pug that they hustled indoors very quickly. What were they up to anyway? He was so busy with his thoughts as he mowed the lawn that he did not hear the stifled giggle on the other side of the hedge. When he came back for another cooky and more lemonade, the cooky plate was empty and the lemonade jug was gone.

Pug went out to the walk and looked up and down the street. People were beginning to crowd into the church sale, but there was not a soul in sight on the side street near the Bailey place. Nothing but a big shepherd dog barking his head off at the end of the hedge next to the garage. Pug walked softly along the hedge and around the corner. The dog made a dash for the space between the garage and hedge. Pug saw a small bare foot reach out to push him back.

"Okay, kids, come on out of there," Pug called. "I see you. I want Mrs. Bailey's lemonade jug. Then beat it back to the social."

The big dog had succeeded in pulling one boy out by the seat of his pants. Two others followed. The largest of the three young ones had the jug under his arm.

"Come and get it!" he challenged. He turned and ran toward the church with the other two yelling behind him. The shepherd dog bounded beside them, barking.

Pug followed fast, but they had a head start and were already mingling with the group on the church lawn as he ran up. He saw the oldest boy duck down and roll the jug under one of the tables. Then the three of them, screeching like banshees, sought the protection of a tall, spare woman at the candy table.

"Hush, boys," she said sharply. "What's the matter now?"

"He's chasing us, Mom. He's chasing us," the oldest one yelled.

Their mother looked around, but Pug had dived under the table to retrieve the jug.

He emerged with it under his arm. "It's Mrs. Bailey's," he mumbled, and fled.

Priscilla and Helen were just leaving the house when he got back. Mrs. Bailey had come out onto the front step with them.

"If you happen to have anything really old in the attic — like an authentic dough table, or some good pewter," she was saying, "I know I can get a good price for it."

"There's nothing like that left in the attic at Dibble Hollow." Helen was gloomy. "When Miss Woodman told us those old, old things were called antiques and people paid outlandish prices for them just because they were scarce, I went right up and looked in our house. There weren't any."

Mrs. Bailey nodded. "It's hard to find good pieces any more. Miss Woodman is right about the craze for antiques. Really old things with the maker's signature on them are scarcer than hen's teeth today. That's the reason I could get a real good price for whatever you have."

"We might have something in our attic," Priscilla reflected. "But I'd have to ask Grandpa before I did anything with it. And he probably would throw a fit."

"He might think it the lesser of two evils — to sell furniture rather than lose the farm."

So that's what the girls were up to — selling antiques! Pug went back to work without having been noticed. He was glad the word had been spelled out for him; he would never have known what an antique was. Dough table. Miles had mentioned his mother's old dough table in his diary and again that very morning. It was in the hideout.

I've just got to locate that hideout, Pug said to himself. "That must be why Miles keeps after me to find it. That's what he meant about the girls giving their eyeteeth for the stuff he and Eb had in there."

Pug was so impatient to look for the hideout that he thought the day would never end.

CHAPTER 13

The Fight

AT THE SUPPER TABLE that night Helen asked Pug what he had been doing "running around with Mrs. Bailey's water jug." Pug told of his experience with the Pratt children.

"Oh, those Pratt kids," Helen said. "Ernie too. He was out snooping around Twin Maples when Prissy and I got home this afternoon. He must have biked out here right after upsetting your apple basket. I saw him talking to Jake Holcomb."

"Now see here," Mr. Allen interjected. "I understand how you feel about what's happened. But can't you think of something good about the Pratts, for a change?" Their father's tone was mild, but Pug knew it meant he had had enough of their criticism.

"Well, Ernie is smart," Pug conceded.

Privately he hoped that Ernie was not smart enough to figure out how Jake happened to be working at Twin Maples.

His father nodded.

"They do seem like awful brats though — from away back," Pug could not resist adding. He stressed the last phrase.

Mr. Allen looked thoughtful. "Now there's something to think about," he said deliberately. "Maybe the family *has* built up a reputation over the years for doing things that are not always considerate. So people begin to say, 'If he's a Pratt, expect the worst.' And the Pratt figures, 'I'll do what's expected of me.' But suppose people expect something *different* from a Pratt. Then —"

"I see what you mean, Dad," said Pug. "You don't have to draw a diagram."

"Then try expecting something good from Ernie, for a change. See what happens," his father suggested.

Pug shrugged. "What could I lose — but my two front teeth or something like that! Only I probably won't see much of him — if I can help it."

"If we ever decide to live here permanently, we're not going in for hates and grudges. They ruin digestions and morals and even lives."

"I don't hate Ernie or anybody, Dad," Pug replied. "I don't even really know him."

He swallowed the last of his milk and got up from the table. "I'll think about what you said, though.

Believe me, I'd try anything if we could stay here. Can I go up on the hill?"

"Not as far as Billy Goat Hill, Pug, only the hill behind the house," Mrs. Allen said. "It's late."

"I don't even know which one *is* Billy Goat Hill."

Even with her mouth full of cake, Helen managed to look superior. "I do," she said.

"I'll bet."

"Billy Goat Hill is the one on the Smith side of the road, nearest the river. Half of it belongs to the Smiths and half to us. Priscilla told me," she explained to her mother.

Pug was disappointed not to be able to explore it that night. But at least he knew now which one to head for in the morning. Tonight he'd look over the hill behind the house.

Pug was so preoccupied that he did not see the shadowy figure by the barn until he was almost there. With a start he recognized Ernie Pratt.

"Hey, what're you doing here?" Pug demanded.

"Nothing. Want to make something of it?"

"I might. I owe you something for dumping those apples."

"You asked for it."

The answer brought Pug up short. He *had* practically dared Ernie to do something, so Ernie had done it. Just what his father had been saying! But how could you help it when someone always had a chip on his shoulder, like Ernie?

"I found out today what you're up to," Ernie

boasted. "Pop would be sore enough to lick you if
he knew."

"It would take more than your dad to lick me."

"Hah. I could do it myself with one hand tied."

"Like fun you could."

"You don't think so?"

"Just try it."

Forgotten were his father's words, as he flung the
challenge.

Before Pug knew how it happened, Ernie's fist
hit him in the stomach. The sudden sight of Miles,
sitting cross-legged on the woodpile, with a grin
lighting his face, helped to throw Pug off balance.
In any case, Ernie's right, following his left, caught
Pug on the chin and threw him back.

In spite of his anger, Pug was impressed.

"Wow! You're lightning, Ernie!" he gasped. "Do
you know you're the first person who ever hit me
unless I let them?"

His voice expressed such genuine admiration, that
Ernie fell back. Suspicious but uncertain, he looked
at Pug.

"No kidding," said Pug rubbing his chin. "You're
the fastest punch thrower I ever saw. I'd like to know
if you could do it again. Come on. Let's see."

His tone was friendly.

The look of amazed disbelief on Ernie's face made
Pug laugh out loud.

"Watch out, here I come," he warned mischie-
vously. He danced around Ernie, who also began to
circle and feint.

This time Pug landed a couple of good punches on Ernie's chin, but he took two in return that made his head bob. It wasn't just because of Miles on the woodpile, either, though he sat there laughing. Ernie was fast — just as fast as he seemed with that first cross. And he was enjoying the tussle as much as Pug. Neither of them noticed Helen come out and then rush back into the house to call Mr. and Mrs. Allen.

But even the absorbed boxers could hear Mr. Allen's stern command, "All right, boys. That's enough."

Pug and Ernie backed off from each other, breathing hard.

"I'm disappointed in you, Pug," Mr. Allen said sternly.

"It's okay, Dad," Pug gasped. "Ernie's a whiz with his fists. We were just having fun. Weren't we, Ernie?"

"Yeah. I can usually hit a kid anywhere I want to. But Pug is fast. Yeah, we were just having fun." Ernie's expression was such a mixture of surprise and delight that all the Allens laughed and he joined them.

"Well, be in by dark." Mr. Allen took Mrs. Allen by one arm and Helen by the other and led them indoors.

Ernie went to the woodpile and got his bicycle. He bent over the handlebars, adjusting the bell.

Pug followed him, kicking at the chips by the sawhorse.

"I wasn't going to tell Pop about Jake Holcomb," Ernie mumbled.

"What are you doing tomorrow?" Pug asked abruptly.

"Nothing much."

"Can you get away alone without any questions being asked?"

"Sure." Ernie was trying hard to mask his eagerness.

"I'm going exploring on the place here. Want to come?"

"What time?"

"Right after breakfast. We eat about seven."

"Okay. Where do you want me to meet you?"

Pug looked surprised. "Right here at the house, of course."

Together they walked down the drive to the road.

"You don't need to worry about my saying anything to anybody about you and Jake Holcomb," Ernie said quietly. "I — I hope old Grandpa Smith gets to keep his farm — even if I would practically give my right arm to live out here in the country."

He jumped on his bicycle and pedaled away fast.

Pug stared down the road after him. I guess you just have to hand it to Dad for knowing how a fellow feels, he thought.

Miles jumped down from the fence right beside him.

"Are you going to let him in on the hideout?" he asked.

"Maybe. When I find it."

"I never thought a Pratt would see the inside of Eb's and my hideout. But you will need help to haul out the heavy things."

"Miles, are you sure you didn't go up that way to hide the money?"

"Dead certain. Haha! Excuse the expression! The ledge there is all rock and no real trees. I know I put the pouch of money in the roots of a big tree."

"What road did you take to the bridge?"

"This one. It was the only one."

Pug sighed. "Well, Mom always says when you lose something go back to where you were before you lost it and think of all the places you've been."

"I will go over the ground again," Miles promised. "But Mr. Miller has been sick. He's not long for this world so I spend much of my time with him. I may even learn to play the bagpipes for him."

"The bagpipes!"

"He said he did not really appreciate my mouth organ music — but he could stand anything on the bagpipes."

"That's a break," Pug laughed.

"One thing I am good at and that is march time. One — two — three — four. And Mr. Miller says when he gets his marching orders, he would like to swing his kilt to the skirl of the bagpipes — whatever that means."

Before Pug could reply, Miles had vanished into the night.

CHAPTER 14

The Hideout

ERNIE WAS WAITING with his dog Shep on the back porch the next morning promptly at seven o'clock.

Pug couldn't help wondering how much of their breakfast conversation he had heard before they knew he was there.

Helen had just asked, "Mother, if we had any antiques, would you sell them to save Twin Maples?"

"I think I might. I suppose it could be a different matter if I knew I actually owned a particularly lovely piece."

It was then Pug noticed Ernie at the door.

"Hi," he called. "Be right with you."

"We're going to explore," he announced as he slapped some bread and cheese together and thrust it into his knapsack. He had already stowed a flashlight and a long piece of clothesline.

"Not on Mr. Smith's property, Pug."

"Give me credit for a little sense, Mom." He waved good-bye. "I don't know how long we'll be gone."

Mrs. Allen laughed. "That bread and cheese won't keep you away forever. When do you have to be home, Ernie?"

"Mom doesn't care if I'm gone all day."

"Be home by suppertime, then, Pug."

Pug was surprised that Helen did not coax to go along. But he soon forgot her in the pure pleasure of the early morning walk as they cut across the road and through the Dibble fields toward Billy Goat Hill. Once or twice he stole a look at Ernie and saw that he was as content with their excursion as Pug was. They said little, but the silence was comfortable.

Once Ernie remarked, "This used to be honest-to-goodness Indian country."

Pug, who was in the lead, looked back and grinned. "We could throw them off our track by wading the creek," he suggested, "if I could find the creek. I know it comes down from Billy Goat Hill, and I know it goes under the road on Twin Maples land, so I didn't dare start from there."

"It's right ahead of us. See how the bushes grow

together? Let's go. I guess the dogs won't lose us even if we wade."

They could hear Shep and Ricky somewhere off to the side. Ernie found the clear brook and the boys waded until they came to a waterfall where a rail fence had caught enough branches and leaves to make a dam. They stepped out of the water and climbed over the fence as Shep and Ricky came bounding down the hill through the underbrush.

"This is the second fence and stone wall we've come to," Pug said. "Let's climb for a while. I bet we could see the river from that ledge up there."

"What are we waiting for? Pneumonia?"

They were both breathing hard when they got to the top of Billy Goat Hill among the high table rocks. Even the dogs were glad to lie down, panting, while the boys rested. As Pug had predicted, they could see the river far below.

He saw something else, which he had not expected to find so soon. His heart beat faster as he realized he was looking right at the four-stone marker pointing to Miles' and Eb's secret hideout.

This was the crucial moment. Should he trust Ernie all the way?

At that moment Ernie, looking down at the swift river and across the valley to the blue hills, said wistfully, "Don't you wish things could always stay like this? Pop is talking about progress all the time. But I like it this way."

Pug got up from the rock where he sprawled. "Yeah, you said it."

He started toward the four huge stones piled on each other and climbed the towering rock formation beside them.

"Can you keep a secret?" he asked.

Ernie nodded eagerly. "I can be as mum as a mummy."

Pug raised his right hand. "Swear you won't tell about what I show you?"

Ernie raised his hand too. "I swear." His voice had sunk to a whisper.

Pug saw that a crevice split the table rock they were on from a ledge a few feet away. On his hands and knees he moved slowly along the edge of the crack until he saw where it widened. Here there was enough room to lower himself between the rocks. He was glad that he had a flashlight. With it he examined the crevice. When he saw the old bean pot at the bottom of the hole he knew that he had found the hideout.

Pug lowered himself carefully between the rocks, making sure he had a good handhold before letting go. It was not as much of a drop as he had feared. He looked up triumphantly at Ernie who was peering eagerly over the edge.

"It's okay," Pug called softly. "Come on down."

He shone the flashlight around at a dry cave room furnished with a couple of ladderback chairs, an old dough table, a small chest, some pewter, and a pair of old brass candlesticks.

"Wow!" Ernie exclaimed as he dropped down beside Pug and looked around. "What a hideout! Whose is it?"

"Years ago it belonged to old Mr. Smith and one of my ancestors," Pug said. "Anyway, finders keepers."

He pulled out the bread and cheese and they sat carefully in the old chairs to eat and to gloat.

"I wouldn't trade this for a million dollars," Pug said.

"Me either."

"But I want to get this dough table out of here for Helen and Prissy. That's what the rope is for. But remember we don't want them to know where this place is!"

Ernie grinned. "You said it."

"The girls may need the chest too," Pug went on. "But we can build things to use here in the hideout. This table and chair are antiques. Helen says they can get quite a bit of money toward the mortgage." He paused and looked straight at Ernie. "Have you got anything against helping us pay it off?"

Ernie looked uncomfortable. "No, Pug. I wish I could change Pop's mind about Twin Maples. But when he gets an idea, he's stubborn as a mule. He honestly does think Mr. Smith would be better off if he was taken care of in a home." His tone was apologetic and pleading at the same time. "He really does believe that," he repeated. "Pop has been okay to me even if he is my stepfather, and I wouldn't like to do anything against him. But I hope Mr. Smith can get the money to pay him," he finished defiantly.

"Don't worry. He's going to," Pug promised. "Come on, give me a hand with the table. We don't dare stay here too long today. Helen would beat an Indian trailing me if she set her mind to it."

With considerable sweating and grunting the boys got the dough table in its sling and up through the cave entrance. Between them they carried it carefully through the tall trees along the firewood trail.

Mrs. Allen was almost as excited as the boys when she realized what they had brought home. Pug, glad Helen was not there, explained to his mother and father where they had found the table. Neither of his parents questioned him too closely in Ernie's presence.

Not until he had waved good-bye to Ernie, and they had promised to get together the following day, did Pug tell them how he had happened on the hideout. He ran upstairs and got the diary to show them.

"Here, the diary of Miles that I found! But the diary and the hideout are strictly for boys," he finished. "Ernie and I don't want Helen and Prissy poking their noses into it."

"They won't bother you; they're completely absorbed in the old furniture project. Would you like them to dispose of this table, Pug?"

"That's what I hunted it up for. There are a couple of candlesticks and a pitcher and two old chairs and a chest besides. But I don't want Helen knowing where they came from. They may not be worth anything anyway. They look junky to me!"

His mother put her hand lovingly on the old table. "The girls have been getting help from Miss Woodman. They also have a book from Mrs. Bailey showing them what to look for," she said. "You can look through that and then check to see if the things in your hideout look like anything in the book."

Helen squealed when she saw the dough table.

"Mother, it's just what Mrs. Bailey asked for!" she exclaimed. "Where did it come from?"

"No questions to be asked and none answered," Mrs. Allen laughed. "Not if you want the table."

Helen was torn between her desire for the table and her curiosity. She finally said, "All right." But she looked suspiciously at Pug. "I suppose you found it if I'm not supposed to ask. Is there more where this came from?"

"Could be."

"Oh, Mother, he's impossible!"

"You've got a nerve," Pug exploded. "Here Ernie and I work all day to get you a valuable antique and you say I'm impossible." He mimicked her tone of exasperation.

"Ernie and you? Worked all day?"

"That's what I said."

"Well, well, well."

"What do you mean by that?"

"Nothing. Just well, well, well."

"Yeah, and you look like Columbus discovering America."

"Do I? Maybe I have," she said sweetly.

Pug was a little surprised that it was his father who laid down the law then.

"Helen, you are to leave Pug strictly alone on this."

"Oh, all right."

Pug was worried when Helen gave in with no more argument than that. She generally hung on like a puppy to a bone.

Still, it seemed the next morning that he had worried about nothing. Helen went off with Priscilla. Pug and Ernie brought the two ladderback chairs from the hideout in the middle of the afternoon. Ernie was unhappy that he had to leave. "I have to be back in Smithville for a three o'clock dentist appointment," he told Pug.

"If I don't show up, Pop will look into it. Then good-bye to this kind of fun for me."

"Jeepers. We don't want that. Go along, Ernie."

Pug waved him on his way home and went back into the house. A note on the kitchen table said his parents had gone grocery shopping in Smithville.

Pug's heart thumped as he realized there was someone moving about upstairs. His first impulse was to bolt out of the house. Instead he mustered his

courage and crept quietly up the steps. Miles never
made that kind of noise, he thought. The noise
seemed to be coming from his own room. Silently Pug
inched his way across the landing till he could peek
in.

"Helen, for the love of Mike, what do you think
you're doing!" he shouted.

His sister was standing on his bed trying to get
Miles' portrait off the wall. But at Pug's cry of in-
dignation, she jerked back and brought the whole
thing down with a crash on top of her.

"Now look what you made me do." She started to
cry.

Pug was afraid she was hurt. When he found she
was not, he really sizzled.

"What *I* made you do!" he yelled at her. "Look at
the back of that picture. It's broken clear across. The
painting itself had better be okay or your name will
be mud."

He picked up the painting and examined the front
carefully. It was all right.

Helen started to cry again.

"Oh, turn off the waterworks," Pug said in a calmer
voice. "And just tell me what you thought you were
doing."

"I was just looking for clues," she sniffled.

"Clues! For what?"

"For where you got that dough table — that's what.
I know you must have found some secret paper or

something. And I just thought you might have hidden it in the back of the picture."

"Why?"

"I couldn't find anything any place else," she confessed in a small voice.

Pug's anger ebbed as he looked at his sister. Maybe he had been selfish about the diary and everything else. But he sure didn't want Helen to move in on that hideout!

"Well, if I found anything I wouldn't put it in the back of a picture," he said, turning the portrait on its face. One side of the broken back came off in his hand. Under it was a packing of yellowed newsprint. *Milltown News* caught his eye.

"Wow!" he said. "You may have found something after all, Helen!"

She stopped crying and bent over the old frame as eagerly as Pug. Carefully they pulled the paper out. It was dated September 10, 1900.

"It's just an old newspaper. I don't see that it tells any secrets about the house or anything," said Helen disappointed.

"This is interesting, though," Pug replied. "We'll keep it out and show it to Mom and Dad. Look at this story about an unidentified kid our own age who was drowned. They think he was carried down Tumbling River from here to Milltown."

Pug stopped reading. This was what Miles meant by the joke on the family! The story about the boy who was buried in the Gideon Miller plot had been in a newspaper used as backing for Miles' own portrait. And the family had never known about it!

"Helen, this might be *it*," he said.

"Might be what?"

"What happened to Miles Dibble."

She grabbed the paper and read the account herself. When she looked up, her eyes were shining.

"We *might* have something," she said eagerly. "And I'm the one who found it. Wait till we show Mom and Dad."

Mr. and Mrs. Allen read the old newspaper with interest. They agreed with the children that the boy might possibly have been Miles.

"If it was Miles, and he had the money from the fair with him, then it looks as if it all went into the river with him," Mr. Allen speculated.

"And that doesn't help one bit with the mortgage," Helen wailed. "Even though the Twin Maples farm looks lots nicer and people are noticing it."

She was right on both counts.

All too soon, it was the day before the mortgage was due. Dinner at Dibble Hollow was a sober meal. Even Helen was pessimistic. What she and Prissy had collected was far short of the amount needed.

"Priscilla has it all in the bank and she's going to tell her grandfather about it tomorrow when he goes in to pay the interest. But from what she's heard, she doesn't think Mr. Pratt has changed his mind," she said dejectedly.

Pug wandered out to the gate after dinner and looked down the road toward Twin Maples. He could not believe his eyes! There came Miles, running as he must have run on that night in 1900, for his very life.

As Miles came up to Pug he panted, "Did what you said. Started at the fair grounds. I've got it, Nathanael! A hundred running steps to the left of the barn, between the big maple roots and the stone wall! I wish I could watch you find it. But I have to be in Milltown at eleven o'clock tonight. Mr. Miller has his marching orders."

"Miles, wait! Wait!" Pug cried but Miles had sprinted on up the road and vanished.

He jumped as Helen said at his elbow, "What are you yelling at?"

He turned on her. "Is there any law against yelling in the country? Why don't you get lost, Helen? I've got things on my mind."

"Oh, well. If that's the way you feel I won't show you something special I got today."

"Like what?"

"Just a present Miss Woodman gave me for my hard work." She started toward the house.

"Hey, wait. What was it?"

"I thought you had other things on your mind."

"So I have. But I wouldn't mind seeing your present from Miss Woodman," he said kindly.

"Don't be so noble. You know you'd give plenty to see it. She gave one to Priscilla too."

"Can't be so precious if she had two."

"That's what you say. Maybe the notes aren't precious to anybody but Miss Woodman — not even to her because she said they were just gibberish — but Eb Smith passed them to her in school and she kept them all these years and gave them to us because we worked so hard for him. And the little chests to keep them in are just darling!"

Notes from Eb to Fanny? Miles had spoken of that. What had he said? Pug suddenly remembered — Miles had grabbed the note in which Eb had given Fanny the key to his code. No wonder Fanny could never make head or tail of them.

"Let's see them," he said as casually as he could.

"Oh, no — not unless you let me in on your plans."

"Your old notes might not be worth the paper they're written on."

"Your plans might not be either. But I'll take a chance and trade even."

"Okay," Pug agreed finally.

He followed Helen to her room. From a small inlaid box she took a folded sheet of yellowed paper.

"Maybe it doesn't make any sense," she said. "But it's a real sure-enough note from Mr. Smith, Miss Woodman said."

Pug tried to disguise his excitement as he looked at the string of letters. "Looks like a code of some kind," he said. "Maybe it's one of the easy ones. Want me to work on it, Helen?" He could not keep the eagerness from his voice.

"If you tell me what it says — if you can work it out." She was as excited as he was. "And don't forget. You said I could be in on your plans too."

"Okay, okay. Give me a few minutes alone so I can put my whole mind on this."

He took the note into his own room. It was in Miles' and Eb's code! Easy to work out since he already knew the code. And it raised his excitement to fever pitch.

> *Miles saw me give you a note. He is mad because I told you our code. I found your hair ribbon that you lost. It smells like you. I keep it in our old maple tree wall safe that we don't use any more.*

The maple tree wall safe! That could agree with the directions Miles had just given him. He could not tell Helen that, but he could take her with him to look for the treasure. He would let her think it was this note that had steered him there.

Helen seemed more excited than Pug was, and he had to warn her to quit hopping around or she would give the whole show away.

They decided to wait until Mr. and Mrs. Allen were asleep.

"I'll climb down the cherry tree," Pug told her. "Can you make it?"

She nodded. "I'll wear my jeans. I can climb as well as you can."

Helen was right. She did get down the tree easily.

Then she and Pug walked in silence from the foot of
the cherry tree to Twin Maples. They went over the
fence instead of risking the creaky gate. They tiptoed
past the Smith farmhouse, and headed for the barn.
From there, Pug started left, counting steps as he ran.
He was up to ninety — almost at the maple tree, when
a figure emerged from the shadows. "Stop where you
are!" cried a deep voice. It was Eb Smith, and he
advanced threateningly.

"Mr. Smith, please let me explain," Pug begged.
"I'm here for your sake. Honest!"

Mr. Smith did not lower his raised cane.

"I want to look for the money you and Miles Dibble were taking home for your brothers."

"At your old tricks again, eh?" It was almost a
snarl. "The villagers been telling you about me and
Miles."

"Well, yes. And I think I know where the money
might be."

"Poppycock!" the old man growled, and spat to
one side.

Pug looked around for Helen and saw that she
had run toward the Smith house. Probably to get
Priscilla.

"Listen, Mr. Smith," he said urgently. "The night
you were followed, didn't Miles wear a white shirt
and bow-tie and high-top button boots with socks
that had stripes running round and round? Maybe a
button or two busted off on one side of his pants so
he had to tie them with string?"

Slowly the raised cane was lowered. Mr. Smith backed away. "Boy, somebody in your family knows what happened that night, same as we always suspected."

"Let me look at the base of that tree, Mr. Smith, or at least look yourself," he persisted. "No one wants to see you lose your farm."

"A fine time to think about that."

"Grandpa, what is it? What are you doing out here in the damp?"

Pug saw Priscilla running toward them with Helen.

"What is it?" she repeated as they came up.

"He wants me to dig at the roots of that maple," muttered her grandfather. "Says the gold that Miles and I fetched from the fair is hid there. Daft!"

"It can't do any harm to look, Grandpa." Priscilla was plainly excited.

"He might not have had much time to hide it, if he was running," Pug explained.

"Well, what's stopping us?" Priscilla cried.

With a quick glance at Mr. Smith who seemed unable to make up his mind, Pug shone his flashlight between the maple and the wall and started to dig. The three of them dug feverishly all around the tree. They found nothing.

"What did I tell you?" Mr. Smith growled. "I looked in that old hiding place the day after the fair. You young jackanapes! You ought to be ashamed to make sport of a man with his back to the wall. For the last time, I tell you, get out!"

"I don't understand it, Mr. Smith."

"Get out!"

Priscilla clung to his upraised arm and waved to Pug frantically to do as her grandfather ordered.

Pug and Helen left reluctantly. They were so disappointed that Helen sniffled most of the way home. Pug would not answer a single one of her questions.

"Go to bed and forget it," he told her at the foot of the stairs. "I am."

CHAPTER 15

Pay-off

PUG FOUND IT EASIER to say he was going to bed and forget than to do it. He slept fitfully, dreaming that men came and moved in on Twin Maples, and that Priscilla was led away in chains by Mrs. Pratt and four bawling children.

He woke suddenly just before dawn, and knew immediately that Miles was there.

Deliberately he turned his back.

"Where's the money?" Miles asked eagerly.

"What money?" Pug retorted.

"What's the matter?" Miles was anxious. "Couldn't you find it?"

"With those fake directions? Who could?"

Miles said nothing, and Pug turned over to look

at him. He was sitting with his head in his hands.

"I have been like a hen on a hot griddle these past weeks," he sighed wearily. "I thought I could leave you to this task while I visited Gideon Miller. He turned sick just after his birthday festivities. I have loyalties there too, you know. I figured you could follow a few simple directions. I thought you trusted me." He raised his head and looked at Pug reproachfully. "First it was Eb lost faith — and now you, one of my own blood."

"I looked where you said and there wasn't a nickel," Pug told him.

Miles looked so puzzled that Pug began to wonder.

"Didn't you say a hundred running steps left of the old barn?"

Miles nodded.

"Left of the barn," Pug repeated. "Left!" Then he sat bolt upright. "Of course! I should have remembered the strawberry patch, and your directions for finding the well. How stupid can I get?"

Miles gaped at him. "You are daft, aren't you?" he asked anxiously.

"I've *been* daft! What time is it?"

"Five o'clock."

Pug jumped out of bed, threw off his pajamas, and began climbing into his clothes. He was shivering with excitement. "I forgot you don't know your right hand from your left — I hope. And those are *twin* maples — *one on each side of the barn*." He laughed nervously. "Thank goodness for that note Eb sent to Fanny Woodman."

He stopped dressing and turned to Miles, "That tree last night. Grandpa Smith said your old safe was there and he had already looked in it."

"I had looked in our old safe myself. What is the matter, Nathanael? Did you mistake my directions?"

"Yes! Now we'll have to move fast. And I have to get Dad in on this."

Pug rushed into his parents' room and shook his father's shoulder. "Dad, Dad, wake up!"

Mr. Allen opened one eye. "For the love of Mike! It's not light yet. What's the matter?"

"It's Twin Maples, Dad. I think we can save it if you'll help. Please!"

Mrs. Allen had slipped into her dressing gown. "What can we do, Pug?"

"I think I know where the money is hidden," Pug said. "But Mr. Smith will shoot me on sight, so I have to have Dad along to tell him we're not fooling. It's our only chance."

While he was talking, Mr. Allen was pulling on his bathrobe. "Pug, how can you possibly know? I don't think we have any right to bother Mr. Smith."

"Please, Dad. You know Miles' diary? That code he and Eb had? Well, Helen has a note from Eb to Fanny Woodman that she could never read because it was in code. But I cracked the code. I'm pretty sure I know where Miles would hide the money if he had time. If I'm wrong we're no worse off, are we?"

"Maybe!" his father said, yawning. "Give me five minutes and I'll be with you. But we're not going out of this house without breakfast. I've got to be fortified before I face that — that old fire-eater."

"I'll have food for you by the time you're ready," Mrs. Allen promised. "I do hope you know what you're up to, Pug."

Pug hoped so himself. Helen was awake and ready to go as soon as he was. She was excited to learn that her note might help find the money. By a quarter of seven they were on their way to Twin Maples.

Mr. Smith was bringing the milk from the barn as they went in the gate. He plodded toward the house as if he did not see them and called to Priscilla. She appeared with a dish towel in her hand and he gave her the pail.

"Get my gun," he told her, "and go after the sheriff. This property is mine for another couple of hours."

"We have no time to waste, Mr. Smith, if we're to keep it in your name longer than that," Mr. Allen said. "Pug thinks he knows where the gold is hidden. Now I don't know whether he is right or —"

"He isn't," growled Mr. Smith. "And I won't have you looking on this land."

"Then I'm afraid I'll have to stand on our rights for Mrs. Allen, who is a Dibble. As I'heard the tale, a part of that money belonged to the Dibbles, and we have some right to dig for it. If Pug is wrong, we'll put back the dirt and I will promise for him that you won't be troubled again."

"For Priscilla's sake," Mrs. Allen said gently. "She could not bear to leave you."

Mr. Smith glared at all of them. Pug's heart stood still as they faced the old man. Time was wasting.

There was Miles, dancing up and down on the stone wall, wig-wagging with both arms. It was now or never.

"Miles never knew his right hand from his left, did he, Mr. Smith?" Pug burst out. "Wasn't it sort of like color blindness with him? Last night we looked at the roots of the wrong tree. But the other one — it's the same distance on the other side of the barn. Right or left made no difference to Miles, did it?" he insisted.

Mr. Smith stood trembling, with hands clenched. Then he turned abruptly and with a curt gesture, led them toward the other maple tree.

Pug felt hot and then cold all over. Suppose he were wrong again? But he was not really surprised when Mr. Smith himself found the moldy, rotting, leather pouch stuffed between the branching maple roots, under the matted moss.

"No!" he whispered as he lifted it from its hiding place. "No, Miles!"

Mr. Allen sprang to help him as he tottered to a seat on an old stump nearby.

Priscilla spread the dish towel on his knees. Mr. Allen produced a jackknife and finished slitting the old pouch for him to empty it into the towel. They

all stared in silence at the heap of coins, and then started to talk at the same time.

Before he got up from the stump, Mr. Smith said to Pug, "Boy, I'm almost afeared to shake hands, but I'd be proud to. How you come to know about Miles, I can't understand. But I'm obliged to you — not just for finding the gold but for proving Miles hid it. It takes a sore spot out of me. You can be sure your Ma will get the Dibble portion of this," he added.

"All we wanted was to straighten things out so we could be friends the way you and Miles were," Pug told him. He did not think it necessary to explain that by "we" he meant himself and Miles.

"I was the worst of the lot," Grandpa Smith was saying, "doubting Miles like that." His voice was sad. "I should have known something happened to him. He was more to me than my own brother. I wish I could tell him so."

"He knew it." Pug sounded positive.

Eb Smith looked at Pug and frowned in perplexity. "Elisha Nathanael," he said, "I never saw a boy that was any surer about things than you are — unless it was Miles himself."

Pug squirmed. "Well, I found his diary, Mr. Smith, so I knew what friends you were. And besides, maybe I *am* a little like Miles, so I'm pretty sure how he would feel now that you have that money."

Mr. Allen looked at his watch. "We can't waste time," he said. "We have Mr. Pratt to deal with. We haven't even counted the money."

"We'll get Ned Bailey out a mite early," Mr. Smith chuckled. He looked years younger. "No banker's hours for him today. This money has to be counted and put in the bank — for you and me." He nodded at Mrs. Allen. "Then I can write a check for Zeke Pratt."

Ned Bailey, a little grumpy at first, was soon listening intently as the story unfolded and he saw the gold pieces.

"Eb," he said heartily, "I couldn't be gladder if it was my own. With what Priscilla has been putting in the bank from the antiques she and Helen have sold, you'll have enough to pay that mortgage and a nice bit over. And Twin Maples looks better than it has since you hurt your leg, thanks to Nathanael working for me so Jake Holcomb could give you a friendly hand." He turned to Pug. "It's time to tell him, Nathanael." He faced Mr. Smith again, whose sharp glance had gone from one to another as Mr. Bailey spoke. "And to tell the truth, I can hardly wait to see Zeke Pratt's face."

Pug felt the same way. Nor was he disappointed. Mr. Pratt's face was truly a study in astonishment as the check for payment in full of the Smith mortgage was handed to him. Eb Smith made no attempt to hide his satisfaction as he said, "It looks as if I still have a home, Zeke."

What Pug was not prepared for was Mr. Pratt's answer.

"Sometimes kids have sharper sight than us oldsters," he said slowly. "First young Nathanael here — and then Ernie — they tried to tell me you'd be better off where you were. But I honestly calculated you needed the care and companionship you would get in the home, Eb. And Prissy seemed so young for keeping up that farm with your leg not so good any more. Looks as if the kids were right and I was wrong."

Mr. Smith blinked and looked taken aback. Pug watched curiously. He knew Grandpa Smith could hold his own in battle. Would he be equal to a surprising apology like this? It was easy to see it had almost bowled him over.

"Well, now." He cleared his throat and glanced around at the rest of them. "Well, now, Zeke. A man can make an honest mistake. I ought to know! And I don't know but it takes a real man to say so. As long as we're at it, I'd better give in that I've made more'n my share of mistakes this summer! Hope I can make these young ones understand I'm plumb ashamed of my cussedness with them when they were trying to help." He drew his brows together and looked at Helen and Pug. Then he turned again to Zeke Pratt. "Maybe your Ernie could give me a hand now and again. I understand he's partial to the country. You're right; Prissy is young. But Twin Maples is her home while I live, and we have good neighbors, it seems."

"Who hope she will consider our home hers too," Mrs. Allen put in quickly.

When Mr. Pratt had gone, Ned Bailey said, "I told you there'd be a nice bit left over, Eb. Mrs. Allen has a tidy amount too."

He turned to the Allens. "I hate to see you folks go back to the city. Seems as if there just ought to be honest-to-goodness Dibbles at Dibble Hollow. And Smithville High School needs a good teacher." He looked at his watch. "Well, it's time to open the bank for regular business."

"I understand that you are chairman of the board of education for the county, Mr. Bailey," said Mr. Allen.

"That's right."

"Would you consider my application for that teacher's position?"

Mr. Bailey beamed. "Just try me!"

"I'll talk it over with my family then, and —"

The shouts of joy showed there was no need for a family pow-wow.

When they got outside, Pug saw Ernie Pratt fiddling with his bicycle. Pug had only time to say in a low voice, "Come on out tomorrow early. Boy, have I got things to tell you!" Pug was so joyful he almost sang the words. "What a day!"

Ernie nodded, his face alight. "I'll be there," he promised. "Dad told me about the Smith farm and how I might even have a chance to work there some. Everything is A-OK, isn't it?"

"You said it."

"If only the summer wasn't almost gone."

"There'll be others," Pug said. "We're going to live here right along."

"No kidding? Wow!"

Pug felt the same way. He could hardly wait to see Miles that night.

"Well, we did it," Miles said complacently from his usual place on the bed. "And this is the last time we shall get together."

"Oh, no, Miles!" Pug cried. "We'll see each other often! We're staying on at Dibble Hollow!"

"You are, Nathanael. But my work is done."

"We could have so much fun," Pug insisted.

"I'm not asking you to forget me," Miles went on as though he had not heard. "No, not that."

"I couldn't forget you — ever!" Pug interrupted fervently.

"As long as you remember me, you'll remember how a misunderstanding and lack of faith separated good people for years — people who should always have been friends."

"Don't worry," Pug said soberly. "I won't forget you and this summer if I live to be a hundred."

"Well, just promise me to wait until you're almost that old before you tell the story of this summer and me," Miles laughed. It will make a good tale for your grandchildren on Halloween."

His voice seemed to be getting fainter and his

figure was becoming luminous, melting into the moonlight.

"Good-bye, Elisha Nathanael Dibble Allen. Don't waste time pining for me or the summer that is gone." A whisper from the moonlight streaming across Miles Dibble's bed drifted over to Pug. "Think about the year that is coming, with the Dibbles and the Smiths and the Pratts all together again, as they should be."

And that is exactly what Pug did. It was good to be Elisha Nathanael Dibble Allen, with Priscilla Smith on the farm next door, and his friend Ernie Pratt in town.

Pug half hoped he would see Miles again. But then one day he realized that the ghost of Dibble Hollow had really gone for good. It was the day he felt a cold muzzle nosing his hand over the edge of his bed.

It was Ricky.

Pug patted the dog's head and heard the thump of Rick's tail on the rag rug, expressing his complete contentment.

"You and me both," Pug whispered to his dog. "Come on up, boy, and get some sleep. We have things to do tomorrow."